THE HIERARCHY OF NEEDS

REBECCA GRACE ALLEN

Rebecca Grace Allen Enterprises

The Hierarchy of Needs

Copyright © 2015 by Rebecca Grace Allen

Print ISBN: 978-0-9992066-0-7

Digital ISBN: 978-0-9978792-4-7

Editing by Christa Soule

First Samhain Publishing, Ltd. electronic publication: July 2015

CONTENTS

One weekend. No strings. And absolutely no falling in love.

Jamie Matthews is stuck in an epic small-town rut. Failure to launch? She's its mascot. And don't even get her started on Dean. Their hot one-night stand was years ago, but she's still a sucker for his tattoos and wolfish good looks. Giving in to temptation could destroy their friendship, so she needs a way to shake him from her system once and for all.

Dean Trescott doesn't do relationships. Especially since he's already married to his failing family business. Jaime, with her bright future and all-kinds-of-sexy smile, is a reminder of everything he'll never have. He needs to keep his mind—and hands—off her...until she offers him one dirty, wild, rebellious weekend.

Two days out of town. No happily ever after required. That's the plan. Surely they can manage it without developing feelings, right?

The Hierarchy of Needs, book 2 in the Portland Rebels series, is a small town, second chance, friends-to-lovers, steamy contemporary romance featuring some hot kissing in the waves, hair pulling, and a man who is damn good with his hands. Grab it today and let the sexy fun begin.

The Hierarchy of Needs. (ˈhīərärkē of nēdz)

A hierarchy of psychological needs which dictate human motivation: safety, love, belonging, esteem, and self-actualization.

Rebel. (ˈrebəl) Noun.

A person who resists rules or norms.

Defiant, disobedient.

Unruly.

Subverts authority, control, or tradition.

ONE

J amie Matthews paced in the foyer by her front door, as far away from her family as she could get. The house was filled to capacity now that her brothers were home. Two days and it was already too much to handle. Another minute and she was going to strangle someone.

And Krissy was taking forever to get ready.

Trying to corral her impatience, Jamie swung her arms out from side to side. A decade of swimming had hewn them into powerful machines. She'd hoped her shoulders would return to something resembling normal when she stopped competing. No such luck, but she could rock a tank top and jeans like nobody's business, and she had every intention of looking good tonight.

It was the last Friday of September, and the final bonfire of the season. She'd been itching for the escape for hours, wanting to trade the suffocating weight of her brothers' presence for a couple of beers, the roaring ocean and a crackling flame.

Not to mention the fact that Dean Trescott would be there.

Jamie's stomach did a little somersault, which frustrated the hell out of her. She and Dean were just friends now, and good ones at that. Her fluttering pulse was only because he was fun to be around, and she was looking forward to seeing him.

There was nothing wrong with that. Nothing wrong at all.

She bent over to touch her fingers to her toes as feet thundered down the stairs. A pair of sneakers appeared in her line of sight.

"Out of my way, poodle head." The words were accompanied by a rough scratch to her scalp. She snapped her body upward and glowered at her oldest brother.

"Don't call me that," Jamie said, tucking the curls he'd pulled loose from her bun back into place. The ten-year age difference between her and Sean always put them at odds. Despite the fact that they were both adults now, he still made her feel like a child.

She was also the only Matthews child who'd inherited her father's unruly locks, earning her the lovely nickname.

"Call it payback for tying my keys to the wind chime this morning," he said. "Jesus, Jamie. Are you ever going to grow up?"

Jamie gave him her most saccharine smile. She'd been up since five—the result of an internal alarm clock that woke her before dawn even though she hadn't had practice or a meet since college—and had used the extra time to figure out which member of the family she'd be pranking.

Sean was so wrapped up in his fiancée he was obviously the easy target.

"I was bored," she said. "Besides, someone's gotta teach Kim the ropes around here."

The woman in question came down the steps to join them. Kim and her younger sister Krissy were the Matthews' houseguests for the weekend. Their parents were staying at a hotel, but Jamie's mother had insisted on putting the bride and her sister up, saying they had plenty of room.

"I appreciated the lesson, Jamie," Kim said. "But how about we lay off the practical jokes until after the wedding?"

"Where's the fun in that?"

"Jamie," Sean warned.

"Sean," she sang back.

The jokes had never gone too far—good-natured ones she'd played on them in the name of sibling fun. Tape on their light switches. Taking the batteries out of their remotes. Resetting their clocks so they thought they were late for school. It stopped being funny when they hit their teens, but it was Jamie's way of getting hers. Of leveling the playing field when there was no way she could match up to them academically.

She'd fallen out of the habit since they'd moved out, but having all three of them home for the weekend, using the nickname she hated and harassing her over her failure to launch, was enough to trigger it again.

Kim wrapped a protective arm around Sean's waist. Whether it was to comfort him or stop him from throttling her, Jamie wasn't sure.

She let out a heavy sigh. Sean's teasing seemed to bring out the worst in her, but she didn't have to act so childish. She *was* happy for him, after all. She could fight the feeling that she was still the baby in a group full of successful adults.

"Fine," she said dramatically. "No more pranks until after you're married. But only because Kim asked me to."

A creak on the second floor landing drew Jamie's attention upward. Krissy finally hopped down the stairs.

"Sorry I took so long," she said. "I was figuring out what to wear."

Jamie eyed her clothes. White stonewashed jeans and a plaid button-down topped with a bright red vest. Combined with Krissy's huge tortoise-shell glasses, the outfit was almost painful to look at. Jamie hadn't been thrilled with having to entertain Krissy that evening. She was still in college, her outward appearance so odd Jamie was sure they wouldn't have a thing to talk about, not to mention the tiny bit of jealousy she harbored over the place Krissy called home. But she hadn't wanted to argue with her mother when the request had been made, and hanging with Krissy was a way out of this house.

"You look...great."

Good thing Jamie wasn't a Disney character, or her nose would've reached Pinocchio proportions. She snatched her jacket and yanked the door open.

"We're leaving," Jamie hollered past Sean and Kim, hoping her parents would hear. "Bye."

They were out on the porch and heading to the sidewalk before anyone had time to reply. Krissy frowned and looked back over her shoulder.

"I feel bad not staying," she said. "Don't they need our help?"

Guilt flickered briefly. They'd left behind a table covered with seating cards and lobster-shaped lollipops waiting to be affixed together with twine. It was part of the coastal chic wedding theme: the decor was nautical, everything decked out in true Down East flair. They probably could've used another pair of hands, but a break before the festivities began was essential.

Besides, crafts weren't exactly Jamie's strong point. She didn't need a reminder of that.

"Nah," she answered, pulling her jacket on. It was a struggle to fit the denim over her shoulders. "Kim and my mom have it covered."

Jamie fought with the fabric until it stretched into place, then picked up her pace, leading Krissy in the direction of the shore. She looked straight ahead, ignoring the reminders of the seasonal shift she always dreaded: the pine needles making a brittle carpet on the pavement, the pumpkins decorating her neighbors' lawns. Autumn was a time to turn away from everything carefree and buckle down, but Jamie didn't know how to do that. It wasn't like she'd had an actual career to return to when summer ended.

She'd traded lifeguarding at the beach for doubling up on her swim lessons, spending all her time at the community center pool instead of the ocean.

A horn honked as a car passed them. Jamie waved, vaguely recognizing the driver and passengers.

"You seem to know a lot of people," Krissy noted.

"Nah. Just a side effect of having been here my entire life."

Well, not her *whole* life. Technically she'd spent four years of it swimming, partying and occasionally studying at the University of New England before moving back into her childhood bedroom. It had been her only option, since the job she'd gotten at the center didn't pay well. The scenario wasn't ideal, but she'd learned to be okay with it.

It was only when The Three Doctors Matthews flew back to the coop, blinding everyone with their golden lights of achievement, that she doubted herself.

The musky scent of burning wood wafted toward them as they reached the cove. Jamie's skin prickled when she saw an old pick-up truck by the side of the road. It was a red harbinger of the past. One glimpse at it, and she was flooded with memories: night sky, ocean smell, balmy spring air. Beach blankets forming a cushioned barrier between her body and the flatbed. The taste of beer in Dean's kiss.

His eyes on hers, his hands tangled in her hair. Her wrists pinned above her head. An orgasm so intense she still remembered every shuddering detail.

Her skin came alive, little pinpricks that matched the tightening of her nipples. Six years had passed, and even though they hadn't had sex, memories of that night still made her pulse race. They shouldn't have, since Dean had come to her a day later saying it had been a mistake, one born out of hormones and too much beer, and asking, "*We still good?*"

His rejection was like belly-flopping into an ice-cold pool, but

Jamie and disappointment had become old friends at that point, and she'd taught herself how to recover.

She'd blown it off with a smile.

The few remaining months of high school had been awkward after that, but they'd settled into a comfortable friendship once she moved back home. Even started flirting again.

It didn't mean anything. Dean flirted with everyone. His inability to commit was actually something they had in common.

Neither of them did relationships, although Dean's turnover rate was a bit higher than hers. There was always some girl hanging on him, another thing Jamie had learned to laugh at. Sure, it bothered her a little every time she watched him disappear with anyone who flashed him some bare skin, but the competition didn't matter when you weren't even in the race.

The legendary Dean Trescott possessed a charm few could resist, but his flirting was nothing more than words when it came to her.

It was fine. She didn't actually want to go there again and risk fucking up their friendship, but that night with him was something she kept on a high shelf in her head. A decadent reminiscence she retreated to when she was alone.

It got her there. Every time.

She'd never known why his rough grip had turned her on so much, or how his playful tug to her hair became a trigger point, a good kind of hurt that rocketed down between her legs until her mind blanked out. Why his stare had seemed to seize her, her body coming alive with a raw, desperate need she hadn't felt before.

Or since.

Jamie shook the memory off. It was ancient history. One never to be repeated. Still, it would be awesome if they could escape to some kind of alternate universe for something brief, wild and sweaty, then go back to reality and pretend it never happened.

"Who are we hanging out with tonight?"

Krissy's question yanked Jamie back into the present.

"Just my friends," she replied, hoping her blasé expression would mask the restless energy pumping through her. "Three guys I grew up with and have known forever."

The soft hisses and sizzling pops of the bonfire guided her toward where Dean and her friends were sitting. They made a semi-circle by the lifeguard stand she'd spent the summer perched on, a plume of smoke between them spiraling up toward the sky.

Jamie gripped the peeling white wood and swung her body around it, throwing herself into a grand entrance.

"Hello, boys."

Dean had the mouth of an open beer bottle by his lips, but paused when he saw her, his lips curling up into a smirk. His chin was masked by the day's worth of stubble he always seemed to have. His crop of dirty blond hair was cut close on the sides but longer in the front, a few slightly mussed strands hanging down low over his eyes. Every inch of him said confident and relaxed, from his ever-present work boots to the swirling lines of ink that wound like ivy from his wrist to his neck.

He was sex incarnate, a wolf on the prowl in a black T-shirt and jeans.

"Jamie Matthews. My favorite girl."

"Oh, I'm still your favorite, huh?"

She was no more his favorite than the last piece of ass he'd hooked up with, but she liked the nickname nonetheless. She also liked the way his gaze swooped from her face to her breasts and back up again. It was part of the game they played, one she wanted to lose herself in tonight.

He grinned. "Of course."

"Good to know." Jamie dropped to the sand by his side, kicked off her flip-flops and stretched out her legs. "I guess that means I'm entitled to your beer."

She snagged his bottle from his fingertips and took a deep, icy swallow.

"Oh, go right ahead." Dean's voice oozed with sarcasm, but there was humor behind it. He nodded to Krissy. "And who's this?"

"This is Sean's fiancée's sister. She's staying with us for the weekend, and I thought we'd show her how we party down at the shore." Jamie pointed her bottle toward each of the guys. "Krissy, this is Dean, Connor and Mikey."

"Krissy, glad you could join us."

Dean angled an arm out toward the cooler. The move lifted his shirt an inch, revealing a slice of skin. His belly wasn't as firm as it had been back in high school, but it was still sexy to see. As was the soft trail of hair that disappeared into his jeans.

Jamie licked her lips and looked away.

Dean popped open a bottle and offered it to Krissy. She was still standing, looking like she wasn't sure where to put herself.

"Thanks," she replied, finally taking the beer and sitting down.

"No problem. Where are you visiting us from?"

She took a sip and winced. "Manhattan. I'm a theater student at N.Y.U."

Jamie cringed, a move Dean noticed, and she hid her frown with a swig of her drink. Her pipe dream of becoming a fashion designer in New York City was something she hadn't told him about years ago, and she wasn't about to now.

His gaze stayed on hers until Connor cleared his throat. On the other side of their circle, Mikey's mouth was hanging open, and he was all-out staring at Krissy.

Connor gave their wiry, black-haired friend a subtle thump on the shoulder.

"Hey," Mikey sputtered. "Krissy. It's nice to meet you."

Dean chuckled into his beer, and Jamie jammed her elbow into his side. He grunted, then laughed. The warm, low sound made her flush with pleasure. Their eyes met, locking for a beat longer than necessary, and her lungs forgot how to work for a second, her belly going tight on a frozen inhale. Whenever he looked straight at her, the space between them somehow seemed to grow smaller, her body pinned in place even though he hadn't touched her, breath going still as if he had.

Krissy smiled at him, then asked, "How do you all know each other?"

"Detention," Jamie and Dean answered in unison.

"Seriously?" Krissy looked so shocked, it was hard not to laugh. Her owl-eyes centered on Jamie. "You were in detention?"

Jamie raised her bottle in a toast. "I was the only Matthews child to ever end up there."

Krissy's mouth gaped open. "A lot?"

"Once, in tenth grade. We were having a test in history, but I had a meet the night before and didn't have time to study. So I stole the exams off my teacher's desk and threw them out the window when he wasn't looking."

"And you got caught."

"Oh, she got caught, all right," Dean interjected. "And ended up being carted into the South Portland High Slammer, just like the rest of us."

He gave her an appreciative smile, one that said *Good job, Matthews*. Jamie couldn't stop herself from grinning back.

Mikey's hands flew to his chest. "*I* never got detention. I just hung out with them afterward."

Connor chuckled. "This isn't confession, Mikey."

"I know." He frowned and stared at the sand. "Just was making that part clear."

"What did *you* do?" Krissy asked Dean.

"More like, what didn't he do?" Connor said. "Detention was Dean's second home."

"It was yours too, for a while," Dean threw back, then turned to Krissy. "We set off fire alarms and didn't do our homework. We're the bad boys your mother warned you about. Connor even did some time."

"A few hours in the county jail doesn't count as 'doing time'," Connor grumbled. "And it was your fault, anyway."

Krissy's eyes widened even further. "How'd you end up in jail?"

Dean drew up one knee and leaned back against the lifeguard stand. "We made a mess of the sheriff's lawn with my truck. Connor took the rap for it, though."

"Why'd you get in so much trouble?" she asked. "You didn't like school?"

Man, this girl asked a lot of questions. Dean didn't seem to mind, though. He merely shrugged.

"School didn't matter to me. I had a job at my dad's garage lined up right after. But don't knock detention. It's where I learned about Maslow's Hierarchy of Needs."

"I'm not familiar with that."

"It's this theory on human motivation. Our detention teacher read it to us from a book one day. Most useful thing I learned in all of high school."

Connor rolled his eyes, muttering, "Here we go."

"Shut it." Dean nestled his bottle in the sand and pressed his fingertips together, making a triangle out of his hands. "It goes like this. There's a pyramid, and all our basic needs make up the bottom—food, water, air, bodily functions..." He grinned, winking at Krissy. "Sex."

Her eyes darted away, clearly embarrassed. Jamie felt a flash of relief.

"Safety is next. Things that make you feel secure like employment, money, family, health. Then there's belonging, which—" He pointed a finger. "—is not the sappy shit you girls call love. It's having people you can rely on, who you know will be there for you."

"We don't need love to survive?" Krissy asked.

"Not romantic love."

Jamie's stomach twisted, although why she wasn't exactly sure. She was no more capable of romance than Dean was. And candy hearts and roses weren't what she wanted with him, anyway.

"The esteem level is all about respect, confidence and achievement," he went on. "Last is self-actualization, where you've become the most complete person possible. Maslow said few people get to that stage, and that's where the problem is. We strive for something our whole lives, trying to become this perfect version of ourselves, but the reason the pyramid is smallest on top is because almost no one gets there, and if we stopped trying so hard, we'd all be happier."

Connor shook his head, laughing. "I'm not sure that's what Maslow was saying."

"It's the truth," Dean argued. "Life would be a lot easier if people weren't reaching for some unattainable future all the time."

Jamie took a heavy pull of her beer and stared out at the waves. If giving up on the impossible was the key to happiness, she should've been the happiest person around.

Swimming had been her ticket to college. She'd broken a record in the 100-yard freestyle as a junior and qualified for the state championships every year, but what she'd really wanted was to get into fashion.

She'd always liked to draw and play around with clothes. All her notebooks were filled with doodles of outfits, ones she eventually made into a portfolio. She applied in secret to Parsons and F.I.T. down in New York City, sending them her best work, but the rejection letters that arrived a few months later proved she didn't make the cut.

Resigned, she packed away her artwork, dusted herself off and accepted a swimming scholarship, limiting her dabbling with fashion to the magazines she read and what she wore. A liberal studies degree four years later didn't prepare her for much, and since it turned out competitive swimming wasn't an option either —she was good, but she wasn't *Olympics* good—becoming a coach was the obvious answer.

There. Perfectly simple life. Maslow would've been proud.

Krissy cocked her head to the side and looked at Dean. "That sounds like the biggest load of crap I've ever heard."

Dean's eyebrows shot up as he tried to pinch away his smile, but he ended up grinning anyway, especially when Mikey erupted into laughter and crawled around to sit next to her.

"You're awesome," he said. Krissy's blush was as bright as the flames.

Dean leaned over and murmured in Jamie's ear, "Dork love."

His breath was hot, his mouth close. A shudder coursed down her spine.

It's just how he is.

It doesn't mean anything.

Connor's phone rang, breaking the spell. One look at his face and it was obvious who was calling.

"Wifey's on the line," Dean teased.

Connor gave him the finger and stepped away. "Hey baby," he said into the phone.

Jamie smiled. She'd been the one who set him up with her friend Gabriella back in June. A summer-time visitor who'd spent her vacations with her late grandmother, Gabriella was like the sister Jamie never had. She'd returned to M.I.T. to finish her last semester of grad school, but she and Connor were bridging the distance. He was no longer the angry, rebellious kid Jamie had grown up with, doing the nine-to-five at a local web development firm and smiling all the time now.

It was a testament to Jamie's matchmaking skills. Too bad she hadn't been so successful with herself.

Dean drained what was left in his bottle and reached for another, throwing an arm around her when he sat back. It wasn't a big surprise—he got touchy-feely when he drank—but his sudden nearness made her shiver.

"Cold?" he asked.

"A little."

The lie didn't bother her as much once he'd pulled her more tightly against him. Dean was thick, stocky. Six feet of muscle with a bit of cushion on top, like a giant teddy bear with the arms of a rugby player.

She settled into his warmth, ignoring the quiet *mayday* that shouted from her mind. Getting comfortable wasn't a good idea. She'd seen him casually wrap an arm around plenty of other girls in the exact same way, but whatever. It felt too good to be like this. Sand. Beer. Fire. Dean.

Connor returned, his phone still pressed to his ear. "I'll hop on Skype as soon as I get home. Ten minutes." He turned away and uttered a soft "Love you."

Dean covered his mouth with a fist. The word *whipped* came out around a cough.

Connor gave him the finger again, but wore a grin the size of China when he waved goodnight and trudged back to where his motorcycle was parked by the dunes. Dean nudged Jamie's shoulder and jutted his chin toward Mikey and Krissy, who'd started whispering across from them.

"You two need some privacy?" he asked.

Krissy threw Jamie an uncertain glance. "We were going to go for a walk."

Jamie twisted her lips to the side in hesitation. She was supposed to be entertaining Krissy, but that didn't mean babysitting her. The girl lived in Manhattan, after all. And Mikey was about as dangerous as a kitten.

"Sure. You remember how to get back to the house?" When she nodded, Jamie waved her on. "Go ahead. I'll meet you there later."

They unfolded themselves from the sand. Mikey crossed his arms over his stomach, then shoved his hands into his back pockets as they walked off toward the shoreline.

Then it was just Jamie and Dean, alone.

TWO

"How's work going?" she asked.

Conversation. It was a good thing to focus on, and not how good he felt next to her. Or his arm draped loosely over her shoulder, and the tattoo covering every inch of it.

Jamie never had a thing for ink, but she'd always liked Dean's. His were more like art, different from the ugly, garish markings she'd seen on other guys. He'd added to the simple tribal band he'd had drawn around his bicep in high school. Now the length of his arm was adorned with a pattern of swirling lines and jagged edges, all enmeshed with a thin strand of barbed wire. It posed a sharp contrast to his fair skin, lit up like gold from the flames.

He had more tattoos under his clothes—Jamie had seen snippets of them over the years, but never up close. She wanted to drag up the edges of his shirt and study them. To see if the artist she'd once known was still there, hiding on the canvas of his skin.

"Work is the same as it always is. Trying to send the customers away happy. Making sure we get new ones." He frowned. "Avoiding fights with my dad."

He took another sip of his beer. It left behind a slick trail on the curve of his lower lip.

She wasn't staring at it. She wasn't.

"You two not getting along?"

Dean had worked in his father's garage since they finished high school. He never went to college, although Jamie didn't think that was what he'd wanted. It was a subject they danced carefully around.

"We're fine. I'm just not working on cars that much anymore. I spend more time doing paperwork than anything else." He lifted his arm, encouraging her to sit up. "Looks like you're running low."

He reached for a fresh beer and handed it to her. The move effectively ended that line of conversation.

Jamie knocked back what was left in her bottle before cracking open the next one, hazarding a glance at the twenty-four-pack's cardboard casing as she swallowed. A dozen empty ones were already inside it. She wondered how many he'd had.

"What about you?" he asked. "How are things going?"

His words were polite. Restrained. As if they hadn't spent the summer hanging out together. But they hadn't been alone like this in a long time. Maybe he was trying to distract himself with conversation too.

Or maybe it was her wretched, horny imagination.

"Awesome," she said dryly. "My brothers are here. Making me crazy."

"Wedding stuff?"

"Not really," she said, although it had put her on overload lately. Constant calls to the house from the country club's catering manager. Her mother showing off the portfolio of the fabulous photographer she'd hired to come up from Boston.

But it wasn't so much that as it was Sean, Brendan and

Owen, and the reminder of their accomplishments: Dartmouth. Yale School of Medicine. Graduations celebrated with Latin honors and champagne.

They were thriving, flourishing, while she was...stuck.

"Something happens when we're all home," she said, not wanting to uncover that particular wound. "We revert back to children."

"You playing tricks on them again?"

Jamie grinned. "A bit, yeah."

"Siblings. I'd say I understand, but—" He shrugged. Threw her a lazy grin. Dean was an only child. And his parents had split long ago.

"Be glad. I wouldn't wish three brilliant older brothers on anyone."

"Yeah," he said with a hard glance at the fire. "Family is totally overrated."

The edge of sarcasm in his voice was as stiff as the set of his jaw. Lately, Dean looked tired. There was a weight on him now, a heaviness she hadn't seen in the cocky teenager she'd met in the back row of detention.

He was handsome even then, sexy in a way most sixteen-year-old boys weren't. He was a rebel too—tattoo hidden under his sleeve, no interest in school and a smirk that made even the teachers blush. Seeing him walk into her Fundamentals of Art class the next semester had been a hell of a shock, almost as surprising as the handful of photographs he'd pushed across the battered table and asked if she thought they were any good.

They were better than good. They were amazing.

She'd showed him her drawings in return, her hands shaking with the kind of nerves usually reserved for a swim meet. Relief was too weak an emotion to describe how she felt when he paged through them, handed them back and said they were awesome.

Aside from their teacher, Dean was the only person Jamie ever shared them with.

Her artwork wasn't something she wanted to risk with too many people. She told her teammates and parents she was taking the class for the easy A, and she'd never breathed a word of it to her brothers. Good thing too. Her rejection letters would've tipped the scales even farther in their direction.

"They'll be out of your hair in a few days," he said. "And then life will go back to normal."

"Normal. Swim lessons." She stuck out her tongue. "Fall."

Dean laughed. "You got something against fall?"

She lifted her bottle and waved it toward the water. "I'd rather be here. At the beach. Eternal summer."

"But fall means Halloween. Your favorite."

Jamie's face went hot, fire licking the pleased flush on her cheeks. "You remember that?"

Halloween was the holiday she enjoyed the most—a day where she could glam it up however she wanted. It was a detail she was surprised he recalled.

"Oh, I remember," he said. "You showed up in detention dressed as an angel. Kinda hard to forget."

Something changed in his expression. His eyes went darker. Flashed with heat. He crossed his arms, and Jamie's gaze skirted to the thick gathering of muscle at his shoulders, where his collarbone made a rugged line along the V-neck of his shirt. She'd kissed that spot once. Licked and sucked until he'd grunted and a bruise rose up on his skin.

She had to talk. Say something. Anything to stop herself from doing something stupid, like stare at his lips. At the stubble lining his jaw.

Like wanting to kiss him.

"You ever take pictures anymore?" she asked.

It was another subject they cautiously avoided. He'd given up photography the same time she'd stopped drawing, but she'd never known why. She hadn't seen him with a camera in his hand in years.

Dean blew out a breath through his nostrils. "Nah. It was just a kid's hobby."

"You were good at it," she offered.

"You were good at drawing. What happened to that?"

Touché.

"I guess that was a kid's hobby too."

He gazed at her again, and the weight of his stare drew her in. The firelight was gleaming bright enough that she could absorb the rich, vivid green of his eyes. Speckled with gold, rimmed in brown and tipped with a layer of fine, blond lashes, they'd always reminded her of the swathe of ocean over marshland at low tide.

She couldn't help but remember the way they'd stayed trained on her when he slipped his hand into her panties and turned her into a shuddering mess beneath him.

"What?" he asked, his voice soft.

"Nothing."

She wasn't about to say that it was in moments like these when heat seemed to spark in the air between them that she wished they could pick up where they'd left off. That she'd always wondered what it would be like to take him in her mouth. If his eyes would stay on hers or drift closed in pleasure.

What it would feel like when he slid deep inside her.

"How come there's no girl climbing all over you tonight?" she asked. "You lose your touch?"

She wasn't sure why she was asking.

She wasn't sure she wanted the answer.

He shook his head. "Just wanted to be around friends tonight."

Right. They were friends. The fact that he was single for the moment didn't change anything.

An uncomfortable buzz started up in Jamie's head. It was the two beers she'd chugged down in less than a half hour that was making her think like this.

She put her bottle down and pulled the elastic from her hair. Shaking her curls free, she closed her eyes and rubbed her temples, trying to will away the beginnings of a headache, as well as the craving for Dean that would never stay quiet.

A tug to her hair made her eyes spring open, a gasp catching in her throat.

She glanced over her shoulder. Dean had captured a ringlet between his thumb and forefinger. One downward shift and the curl went straight, bouncing back into place when he released it.

He smirked. His eyes flashed. Jamie's skin blazed hot and cold.

Did he know what he was doing? Did he remember this was what set things off a million years ago?

Did he want to do it again?

No, this was drunk Dean. Flirtatious Dean, with no one around to flirt with but her. Uncertainty slithered into a hollow place inside her, a reminder that their teasing in recent years had never once gone past playful banter into something more. She wasn't sure she wanted to test the strength of that ice and risk plummeting into the rejection that could be lying beneath it.

Her fight-or-flight instinct kicked in. She hopped to her feet. The world swayed a little. "I dare you to run into the water with me."

Dean snorted. "No way. It's gotta be freezing out there."

"We're not going surfing, you pansy. Just your feet." She bent down to roll her jeans up to her calves, hair falling over her face as she looked up at him. "Come on, you grew up here. You should be used to the temperature of the Atlantic by now."

He didn't budge. Jamie stood up to her full height, her hands on her hips in a challenge.

"You've gone soft, Trescott. Just like that belly of yours."

His eyes narrowed. "Oh, you are so dead."

He launched up from the sand, kicking off his shoes as Jamie sprinted toward the waves. She could hear his footsteps getting closer, and she ran faster, skidding to a stop when she reached the first lick of the ocean. She threw a leg out to trip him.

Pranks worked better when she wasn't tipsy. She lost her balance and fell ass-down into the water.

Dean's triumphant grin eclipsed the moonlight above him. "Ha! That's what you get."

Jamie grabbed two fistfuls of his shirt and yanked him down into the water with her. He cursed when he landed on top of her, water splashing everywhere.

"Gotchya," she yelled to the stars.

Dean rolled to his side, laughing. "You're nuts, you know that?"

"Yup, that's why you like me."

"True."

His face grew serious, eyes darting from hers down to her lips, then he cupped her cheek in one big hand. Cold saltwater dripped off his fingers and trickled down her neck. Jamie wasn't sure what was happening until he closed the distance between them and kissed her.

Shock hit her like a frigid wave, quickly dissipating as she melted into his kiss. His mouth felt the same as it did years ago— full bottom lip, top soft and yielding. Each time he came back for more, his kisses got rougher, more desperate. Teeth raking. Breath rasping.

She couldn't make herself care why or how this was happening. She just wanted to feel.

Jamie moaned and kissed him back, one wet hand clutching his shirt, dragging him closer. He licked her bottom lip, asking permission.

As if he needed it.

She granted his request with a swipe of her tongue over his. His mouth was hot, his stubble a delicious sharp bite on her chin. Dean groaned and folded his body over hers, pushing her down into the water. She slipped her fingers through his belt loops and pulled him down, clawing. Needing. He grunted when their hips slid together. He was hard already, and she bucked up to feel more of him, wanting to touch, to taste. He ground against her and captured her bottom lip between his teeth, a tiny punishment. She gasped for air, breaking the kiss to whisper his name.

Dean stilled. Completely.

"Jamie. Fuck." His forehead dropped down to meet the space between her neck and shoulder. "Ah, shit. What am I doing?"

Everything inside her froze. She released her grip on his jeans.

"I've been drinking. I don't know what—" He came up on his knees and shook his head. "I'm sorry."

Disappointment choked her, cutting off her air, but she threw on a smile.

"No worries," she said, hoping he didn't notice the way her voice cracked. She picked herself up from the water, her clothes a weight almost as heavy as the sinking feeling in her gut. "I'm sopping wet. I'm gonna head home."

She started to walk, her body numb, eyes focused on the spot where her sandals sat in the sand.

"Jamie, wait."

She turned around, hope a nasty stab in her heart. Dean's shirt was matted to his chest. His arms hung down, limp by his sides. His hair was sticking out in crazy angles.

"I'm really sorry," he said. "We still good?"

Funny how those words sucked just as much the second time around.

Jamie nodded, forcing another wide grin. "Sure. It was the booze talking, just like last time."

"Right," he agreed, eyes solemn. "Just like last time."

She had to believe that, rather than think something was actually happening here. She couldn't make that mistake again.

She snatched her shoes from the ground and headed home.

THREE

"**D**ean, how do you know what to do with girls?"

Mikey's question barely registered. The pounding between Dean's ears was blocking out everything around him. He lifted his head from where he'd pressed it against the passenger side window of his truck.

"What?" His mouth was dry. An unpleasant taste threatened.

"With girls. How do you know what to..." Mikey lifted a hand from the steering wheel and waved his fingers in the air. "*Do* with them."

Ah. His infamous reputation for knowing how to turn a woman on. Exactly what Dean wanted to talk about right now.

"You've gotta pay attention," he replied, then cringed. Talking made his head hurt more. Maybe it hadn't been such a great idea to finish the rest of the beers while he waited for Mikey to return from his walk.

Fuck, he was cold.

"It's like working on a car," he continued. "You listen for the right noises. The right vibrations and movements, and you find what makes them tick."

He was the world's biggest fucking hypocrite. Wasn't it obvious he didn't have a clue how to make anything work, with the way things had gone down with Jamie tonight?

What the hell had he been thinking?

Mikey sighed. "That really doesn't help me at all, Dean. You know I don't have a lot of experience with cars. Or girls."

That was the truth. Mikey's Schwinn had its own parking space in the corner of Dean's loft. And he was pretty sure his buddy was still a virgin.

He closed his eyes and tried to force his brain into action. Mikey needed to know how to get a girl's motor going. They'd been friends since the fourth grade, and the guy had become Dean's personal DD more than once. The least he could do was help out with some advice.

"Every girl has something that sets her off. Dirty talk, kissing their necks—" Dean cleared his throat. "—playing with their hair."

Don't go there.

Keep talking.

"You try out a couple of different things, start out easy and watch how they react. See what makes their eyes go wide, what makes them shiver or gasp, then ramp that shit up. You've just gotta listen until you figure out what it is."

It was the fail-safe blueprint that had worked for him every single time. He had this...*knack* or something. He'd learned to pay attention, to gauge their responses, finding what set them off.

Jamie's trigger? Having her hair pulled. He'd figured that out a long time ago.

"What if you can't figure it out?" Mikey asked.

Dean closed his eyes and rested his temple on the glass. "Then I advise you to not forget about the power of lubrication."

Mikey wasn't laughing. Dean peeled one eye open.

"I take it things didn't go well with Krissy?" he asked.

"Things didn't even 'go' at all."

Poor guy. He'd always been the odd man out when it came to Dean and Connor, trying to figure out how to pass go when the two of them were already at the finish line.

"She'll be around for a few more days. Maybe you'll get another shot," he said. "You're putting too much thought into it anyway. Sex is a biological need. A time to check out and lose yourself to the rush. When you make it into more than that, it stops being fun."

It was another thing that had worked for him. Keeping sex and emotions separate.

He guessed that made two strikes for him tonight.

"Right. Sure." Mikey nodded. "Thanks."

Dean crossed his arms and settled back against the seat. "No problem."

They pulled into the lot by the old waterfront warehouse Dean called home. It was once a building for handling cargo at the height of Portland's shipbuilding age. His father bought it five years ago with a hefty bank loan and a plan to let Dean rent out the second floor, using the space on the first as storage for the family business.

All that was in there now was junk covered in more junk. Dean avoided going down there as much as possible. He avoided his dad's place too.

He flinched when Mikey snapped on the light fixture in the kitchen. The wide-open space echoed with the painfully loud noise of Dean's keys being slapped down on a kitchen counter. The brick walls, high ceilings and exposed pipes didn't do much to absorb the sound of Mikey clomping toward the fridge either.

"Do you have anything to eat other than PB and J?"

It was a given his friend would be crashing here—there was a permanent ass print on his couch from the number of times Mikey needed to get away from his folks after a blowout—but that didn't mean Dean had to play the host. He needed a shower, some painkillers and his bed, stat.

Dean leaned against a wall. "There's some cereal in the cabinet."

"That's it?"

"There might be some milk left too. I don't know, I think I finished it this morning."

"Your diet frightens me."

Dean pushed off the wall. "G'night, Mikey."

Trudging toward the bathroom, Dean pried off his clothes and stepped into the shower. He scraped shampoo over his scalp and rinsed it through, trying to wash out the salt water along with the images playing on repeat in his mind: firelight and Jamie's smile. Her slim hips and firm ass. The soft spill of curls inching down the slope of her neck.

He was a shit. A real grade-A fuckup, because he remembered what happened six years ago, and he'd wanted it to happen again.

He couldn't help himself, not with the way she looked tonight, as fresh-faced as she'd been in high school with a grin that lit up the whole fucking block. She'd been an enigma to him since she showed up in detention, a ray of sunshine trapped between drab walls and fluorescent lighting.

She'd asked if he remembered her on Halloween. As if he could fucking forget.

A white, long-sleeved sweater that set off the olive tone of her skin. Matching leggings that showed off every curve. Shimmering wings, and a halo sticking up out of her headband. There was something in her eyes too—big and brown and sparkling, like she had a secret she wasn't sharing. Combined with those cherubic curls, she'd looked like some kind of deviant angel: innocent, but with a body that had him sporting wood the rest of the afternoon. He couldn't help imagining what that angel would look like with her hand between her legs. A fallen star burning up with pleasure.

Dean's body reacted instantly. It was a fantasy that still woke up his dick nearly every morning.

His brain fast-forwarded to two years later. A ride home after dark had them parked at the shoreline, a six-pack between them in the back of his truck. Tugging her hair had been a whim, something he'd done to tease her. He'd never expected her spine to go rigid, shoulders hiking up to her ears, a shiver rolling through her like a wave crashing on the shore.

Dean rubbed his hands over his face, trying to block out the memory of the moment everything changed between them, but it was too vivid, too clear. He'd wanted to coax that reaction out of her again. To find out how to make a stronger tremor rock through her. To make her eyes grow heavy-lidded with lust.

He found it by pushing that tug in her hair a step further and making a fist. She'd moaned. Lifted her hips. Whispered the word *yes*.

Shit, he'd tried to stop himself, but it was too late. He needed to get off. Now.

Dean groaned and gave in—one slow-fisted pump that sent sparks of pleasure through him. Bracing his other arm against the tile and resting his forehead against it, he let the memories wash over him. Her mouth, hot and eager. Breasts a perfect handful, nipples rising to a rosy pucker under his thumbs. Her head falling back on a gasp when he held her wrists down. The sound she'd made when he brushed his fingers over the damp cotton between her thighs.

The noise had gone straight from his ears to his cock.

Dean's strokes turned fast and brutal, his dick as thick and greedy as it had been that night. He wasn't a virgin, but he'd been far too amped up, worried he'd hurt her. And no one's first time should be in the back of a truck. So he'd spent ages rubbing and teasing her, learning her body like he was learning to drive stick, memorizing every gasp and shiver until her back arched, mouth going slack as she whimpered out his name.

Sensation ripped through him. Dean clamped his eyes shut and pressed his mouth against his bicep, silencing his shudder.

Disgusted with himself, he rinsed his hand and shut off the spigot. He had no business thinking about her like this. There was a reason he'd promised himself to keep his relationship with Jamie strictly in the friend zone, where it belonged. She had a future, a life to live.

He didn't.

Dean stepped out of the shower and snatched a towel. Two painkillers and one heavy swig of water later, he padded down the hall to his room. It was freezing in there, so he grabbed some boxers and went hunting for his sweats. He found them in a drawer, noting they fit more snugly than he would've liked. He had shoulders he was proud of and jacked up arms, but the abs of steel he'd once had weren't as visible anymore—the result of a few too many beers making themselves at home in his gut.

He didn't like it that Jamie had noticed. Cutting back on that shit was definitely going on the agenda.

Still too cold, he pulled one of his heavier Henleys down from a high shelf in his closet. The sleeve got snagged on something. Dean tried to wrench it free but the clothes started fighting back. One strong yank later and a whole pile of crap toppled down and landed in a heap on the floor.

Grumbling out a curse, he began gathering up the mess. Buried under everything, so dark it nearly blended with the wooden slats of his floor, was a thin, flat, leather folio.

Of course he'd have to see that tonight.

Dean snatched it up with the intention of putting it back in its place, but the handle felt heavy in his hand. The contents beckoned him, calling him into a past he didn't want to remember. Tucked inside it were a dozen of his favorite photos.

The kid's hobby he'd given up long ago.

Dean sighed and sank down onto his bed. Sixteen and defiant, he'd thought school was a waste of time. What was the point in studying when he was going to be fixing up cars for the rest of his life? Goofing around instead of doing his homework was what landed him in detention, something he'd mildly regretted until Connor showed up. The kid had no boundaries. He was a powder keg, eager to fight, and Dean fed off that energy. But the persistent misbehavior brought him to an obligatory meeting with his guidance counselor.

She'd looked at him with tired, pleading eyes and asked if there was *anything* other than cars that interested him. Desperate for a way out, he'd begrudgingly admitted that taking pictures was kind of cool.

He wasn't actually invested in it or anything. He only had a camera because his mother sent him one as a birthday present after the divorce, a shiny digital one back when that technology was brand new. It was a gift distant enough that it was obvious she hadn't put much thought into it, but expensive enough that it would seem like she cared.

Dean shifted the portfolio to the side and collapsed back on his bed. His parents had been high school sweethearts, married at eighteen. Mom had big dreams of a life somewhere else, of traveling and seeing the world, but Dad needed to take over the family business when his father suddenly passed away, so she stuck by his side.

Fifteen years later, the business was struggling and so were they. Dean heard them fighting pretty much every night. He came home one day the summer before high school started to find them waiting for him at the kitchen table, solemn expressions on their faces.

Now his mother lived with her new husband in a nice house on the Cape. Dean saw her at Thanksgiving and Christmas.

He had the option of going with her when she left, but he'd wanted to stay in Portland. At the time, he'd been stoked to have a future filled with nothing more than blasting music in the garage and playing with gears and carburetors. It wasn't until he realized he was good at photography that he'd started to think about any other life.

And that, of course, was Jamie's influence.

She never ended up back in detention, so he hadn't seen her again until he'd reluctantly walked into the beginner's art class he'd agreed to take the following semester, a pre-req for photography. Her smile was the only thing cooling his temper when he'd lumbered sullenly into the classroom, ready to bolt or punch someone as soon as the first snicker was thrown his way.

No one laughed. Or if they had, he'd been too busy with Jamie once he sat down with her to notice. Too fascinated with her skill with a charcoal pencil and the human form. What the hell she was doing wasting her time in a pool, he'd had no idea, because her drawings were pretty damn good.

She'd encouraged him too. Her smile pushed him to want to stay there, to actually concentrate for once. Soon he was enjoying the class, learning concepts he'd never spent time with before: color, form, space, texture. Studying the works of Dali, Warhol and Van Gogh. A semester later, he was spending his time in a darkroom instead of detention and showing up late to the garage because he was on the side of the road, caught up by some moment he absolutely had to get on film. And that night senior year when he'd found her without a ride home after practice, he'd parked them by the cove and told her he put a portfolio together. That he'd played with the idea of applying to college after all.

Her squeal of approval had been infectious, and a world of possibilities suddenly opened up to him.

The possibilities had seemed endless that night.

He hadn't realized how badly he wanted her support until he said it, and turned the tables on her then, wanting to know where she was going after graduation. He knew the world she came from—one where going to college was a guarantee. But he'd wondered if there was a chance she'd be sticking around in Portland.

If he had an actual shot with her.

She'd looked up at the sky and said she'd been offered a swimming scholarship, but didn't know if she wanted it. That she had no idea what she wanted at all.

It didn't make sense. She came from a life of privilege, countless choices lined up in front of her, and yet she seemed unable to make one. So he'd tugged on her hair to get her attention. To make her talk. To look at him.

She had, breath catching, her big brown eyes going wide.

Jesus, those eyes of hers. Almond shaped and framed with dark lashes, almost amber when the light hit them right.

He remembered the way they'd pinched shut in pleasured agony when he'd stroked her to her release. How they'd stayed closed for a few breathless moments, and he'd licked her flavor off his fingers, desperate to know what she tasted like. The drowsy way she'd opened them, low-lidded with syrupy satisfaction when she ran a tentative palm over his jeans and asked him to show her what he liked.

She'd been so unsure of herself, her grip under his fingers' direction tentative and slow. Then she'd kissed his neck, scraped her teeth over his skin in a bite just shy of rough, and he'd gone from showing her the ropes to two seconds away from coming in her hand.

Dean was hard again, pulse thundering in his cock.

That shit needed to stop, right the fuck now. Because no

matter how badly he'd wanted to follow through and ask her out again, once he'd dropped her off, everything had changed.

He jerked his thermal over his head, then stood and heaved the portfolio back into its place. The camera was up there too, somewhere. He'd stopped using it after that night with Jamie, when he'd gone home and shown his dad his work, casual as he threw around words like *community college* and *art major* and *what do you think?*

His old man's reply? That photography could be a great hobby and all, but he needed Dean in the shop.

It wasn't like his dad had meant to crush his dreams or anything. They weren't even dreams, really. Just an idea he'd had. Still, having one hand clapped on his shoulder while his father reminded him that his future was in the business, and he needed to make sure Dean understood that, had stung like a bitch.

That was the moment he'd realized starting anything with Jamie wasn't fair to her. He was going to spend his life married to the garage. He was old enough to know the business was in debt, and he needed to make it his first priority. He couldn't give anything to anyone, least of all Jamie.

Especially Jamie.

He wouldn't risk sucking her into the same life his mom had, a wife to someone who spent all his time slaving away, her youth given up to a lost cause, a marriage they never should've had in the first place exhausted years later.

Dean shut off the light and fell into bed, reminding himself of the same shit he had since he was eighteen. One of these days Jamie was going to get out of Portland and make an awesome life for herself. She'd find the right guy, get married and live happily ever after.

It was the best future for both of them. She was everything happy and hopeful, and he'd had his hopes dashed long ago.

That was why Maslow's Hierarchy was still the best thing he'd ever learned.

It taught him how to ignore what he wanted.

FOUR

J amie stayed in her room as long as possible on Saturday morning, her door shut until the sound of starting car engines replaced her brothers' voices. It was almost noon. She hadn't eaten in hours. Her stomach gurgled angrily, but she wanted to stay put a bit longer—a little extra insurance in case they came back quickly.

Face down on her bed, she flipped mindlessly through her October issue of *Vogue*. She always waited until the first of the month to crack her magazines open, peeling back the cover like it was a shiny new present, but today she couldn't concentrate. She couldn't stop thinking about Dean, and what happened the night before. The taste of his kiss, the rasp of his stubble. The low groan that rumbled through him when he slipped his tongue into her mouth.

And then the words *We still good?* echoed through her head.

Embarrassment hit her stomach like lead dropping into water. Jamie buried her face in her hands.

He'd only kissed her because he was drunk. Nothing more to it than that. If anything, she should've been grateful he hit the brakes when he did. He'd stopped things before they went too far, making it clear that their friendship was what mattered.

He valued her as a friend. And if there was one thing Jamie could hold over Dean's one-week wonders, it was that they'd come and gone while she was still in his life.

They'd be able to go back to normal. Whatever weird feelings that kiss had kicked up would fade by the next time she saw him, which wasn't likely to be for a while, anyway.

A quiet knock at the door preempted Krissy's entrance. She popped her head into Jamie's room, her raven hair wound into two uneven pigtails.

"You up?"

Silly question. She'd been up longer than anyone. And she hadn't slept in since the ninth grade.

"Yup. You know where the guys went?"

"To play golf with your dad."

Of course. Because that was what four doctors did when they had a few hours to kill. "Awesome. Come on in."

Krissy closed the door behind her. "You must be proud of them."

"Oh, yeah. Super proud." As if growing up in the shadows of their greatness hadn't been bad enough, Owen was finishing his residency in emergency medicine, Brendan had recently joined a small family practice, and Sean was on his way to becoming as well-known a surgeon as their father.

She was the black sheep in a family of overachievers.

"You didn't want to be a doctor too?"

Jamie snorted. "Wasn't really my thing."

Krissy sat down on the bed, and Jamie gave her a covert once-over. Another plaid button-down, this one blue and gray, worn over a lumpy T-shirt. Faded Chucks on her feet. It could've been an attempt at a geek chic look, if it weren't for the bright red patterned tights and orange pleated skirt she had on too.

The girl was seriously fashion-challenged.

Jamie resisted the urge to give style advice. It wasn't her place to do that with someone she'd known for less than twenty-four hours, even though Krissy was technically about to be family.

"What are you reading?" Krissy asked.

Looked like the Q-and-A portion of the program had begun.

"*Vogue.*"

Krissy's brows bunched down low. "You're into fashion? I thought you were a swim coach."

Jamie smoothed a hand over the glossy cover. She'd been reading it for years, poring over style reports of the newest trends, devouring the images of haute couture designs and timeless looks of glamour.

"I am," she said. "I just like reading it."

And imagining what it would be like to create the kinds of clothes it showcased. The magazine was a portal to another world, one she'd never get to live in but could experience vicariously through posed photographs and perfume samples.

"Do you swim a lot? Being a coach and all?"

Jamie's head spun at the new line of questioning.

"Not as much as I used to, but I still do my laps every day." She paused and scrunched up her nose. "Well, *almost* every day."

She always felt a little guilty when she skipped a workout, but she'd taken the weekend off. Showing up at the center would've only given her boss an opportunity to talk about the Assistant Aquatics Director position he'd mentioned the week before.

Dodging people worked wonders.

"It sounds like a fun job," Krissy said. "Being in a pool all day."

"Trust me, having goggle marks imprinted on your face, super dry skin and constantly smelling like chlorine isn't as exciting as it sounds."

"You don't like it?"

Jamie hesitated before answering. *Liking* swimming wasn't the problem. The pool was the only place she'd felt a sense of accomplishment. There was no comparing her to her brothers when it came to a meet, because you couldn't argue with a clock. They'd tried to race her once, back when she'd made her record. Leaving them in her wake with her legal turns and stroke recovery had felt awesome.

It felt somewhat less than awesome now, since it looked like swimming was going to be all she ever did.

She shrugged. Threw on a big smile. "It's a job."

Needing a subject change, she started to ask how things went with Mikey at the beach, but a sharp rap on the door cut her off.

"Jamie, do you plan on making an appearance at any point today?" her mother asked. "Or will we only be seeing you at the rehearsal dinner?"

The tinge of exasperation in her tone had Jamie closing the magazine and getting to her feet. "Coming."

She and her mother had a decent relationship. They spent time together—usually shopping or having lunch and insignificant conversation during the downtime her mother had in between more important obligations—but for the most part Jamie felt like an outsider in her family.

Each of her brothers' births had been spaced an even two years apart, but she'd come along six years after Owen, and was fairly certain she was an accident. A curly-haired misfit who upset the balance of their perfect little family.

Perfect grades, perfect hair. Perfect acceptances into Ivy League schools.

She'd wanted one tiny accomplishment to set her apart from them, but she'd never been able to keep up, barely scraping by with C's, hiding her frustration in her smiles and practical jokes. She hoped swimming would be her thing, but even that had fallen flat, and since she finished college, she felt almost casually forgotten by her parents. As if they'd successfully fulfilled their parenting roles with her brothers and had done all they could with her.

Of course she was grateful they'd let her live at home rent-free for the last two years. It was something she would've felt guiltier about if they weren't constantly passing off questions about why she hadn't embarked on some noble and important career with a wave of a hand and words like "That's just Jamie. She'll figure herself out eventually."

Downstairs in the kitchen, Kim was putting the finishing touches on a massive salad.

"Afternoon, ladies." She handed each of them a plate. "Krissy, did you tell Jamie how nicely your bridesmaid dress fit?"

Suddenly shy, Krissy shook her head and focused on the food.

"Well, it looked great," Kim continued. "Thanks again for picking them out, Jamie. I think you might have found the elusive dress that doesn't get donated to charity ten seconds after the wedding is over."

Jamie beamed. "Thank you."

She'd sketched the dresses when Kim asked her to be a bridesmaid, then hunted through magazines and websites until she'd found a match. They were sleeveless, navy blue sheaths made from a smooth knit crepe. The surplice neckline dipped down low, the hemlines kissed the spot above the knee. She'd instantly known the dark hue would offset the burnt oranges, buttery taupes and fiery reds chosen for the linens, bouquets and centerpieces.

"Was fashion something you ever thought about doing seriously?" Kim asked.

Jamie's chest went tight, lungs constricting with that familiar pressure, prompting a need to escape. She sat down with her plate and jabbed her fork into a tomato.

"Nah. Not seriously." It was easy to hide the lie as she busied herself with chewing.

"You were more serious about swimming then?"

Yup, that was exactly why she was stalling the discussion with her boss. "I guess."

"Haven't you figured Jamie out by now?" her mother asked as she sat down with them. "She's never serious about anything."

It was said with a smile, but the comment was like being stabbed with a butter knife—not sharp enough to do any real damage, but painful all the same.

"Nope," Jamie said as she punctured another tomato, hoping her smile belied the churning in her gut. "Life's a lot more fun that way."

If Kim noticed any tension, she kept quiet about it. "Well, you should come down to New York sometime anyway," she said. "Maybe during fashion week. You could stay with Krissy and her roommate."

Jamie's heart raced uncomfortably. New York Fashion Week was something she'd always wanted to see, but going there now would remind her of the exciting life she'd never have. She'd sit in the back row and watch, no different than any other tourist.

She wouldn't really *be* there.

"Maybe. Thanks for the offer."

"Sure." Kim smiled, then threw Krissy the oddest glance. A pointed one that seemed to say *now*. When her sister didn't speak, she cleared her throat. "Mrs. Matthews, Krissy has a question to ask you."

Krissy's fork fell to her plate with a clatter. She fumbled to retrieve it.

"I know it's last minute, but I was wondering if it would be all right for Michael Pelletier to come to the wedding as...my date."

Jamie grinned. Their walk must've been pretty interesting. Go Mikey.

"I think we can make it work," Jamie's mother said with a polite smile. "He can always eat standing up."

"Thanks, Mrs. Matthews." Kim's gaze flipped to Jamie. "Hey, how come there won't be a plus-one for you at the wedding?"

And Jamie was done with lunch.

"I wanted to spend the day focused on family."

It was the easiest explanation. Better than saying she'd been weighing her options for longer than she wanted to admit, and still wasn't interested in committing to anyone.

It wasn't that she hadn't liked the guys she'd dated. There'd been some promising candidates, from the captain of the track team she'd lost her virginity to shortly after Dean to the fellow jocks she'd dated in college. There'd been a handful of boyfriends in the years since, but none of them held her interest for long.

Relationships. One more thing she'd never been able to be serious about.

The phone rang. Jamie lunged for it, the escape a welcome relief. She was barely able to say hello before a panicked female on the other end identified herself as the wedding photographer's wife.

"My husband's been in an accident," she said. "Can I speak to Mrs. Matthews?"

Crap. That didn't sound good. At all.

Jamie extended her arm in her mother's direction. "It's for you. I think the photographer might not be able to make it."

Her mother stilled. "Jamie Marie Matthews, you promised. No practical jokes until after the wedding."

"It's not a joke," she insisted. "His wife is on the phone."

Alarm flashed in her mother's eyes. "You're telling the truth."

She nodded and handed the phone over. Her mother took it and walked into another room.

Jamie cleared her place, feeling like she'd taken a dolphin kick to the stomach. She rinsed off her plate, blinking back the sudden sting of tears. Of course her mother would think it was a prank. Her entire family thought she never took anything seriously, too wild and directionless to care. She supposed it was a fact she should've been proud of. It meant she'd become a rock star at covering her feelings of not being good enough, her sarcasm, smiles and humor never making anyone the wiser about how lost she felt.

Her mother returned to the table, phone in hand.

"The photographer and his assistant were hit by a truck when they merged onto I-95," she said. "They're being airlifted to Portsmouth Regional Hospital."

Kim's mouth dropped open. "Oh, that's awful."

Jamie winced. No wonder his wife had sounded so upset.

"I hope they'll be okay," she said, but after years watching her father get similar calls, she recognized the look on her mother's face. Those two were going to be out of commission for a while.

"I hope so too," her mother said. "Portsmouth has a good team. They're in capable hands. However, this unfortunately means we have no photographer. Our contract didn't have an in-case-of-emergency back-up plan, and there's no way we'll be able to find someone else on such short notice."

A knot lodged itself in Jamie's stomach and she let out a sigh. There was one person who might be able to help. Even if he was the last person she wanted to talk to.

"Hold on. Don't panic yet."

She retrieved her phone from her pocket and pulled up Dean's number, last night hanging over her like a storm cloud. Calling him now could look like she was trying to throw herself in his path, but it wasn't as if she could've manufactured this.

She hit send. The call went straight to voicemail. He was probably at the shop, his head bent under the hood of some busted old vehicle. Maybe it would be less awkward if she asked him in person.

"I'm going to call in a favor from a friend," she said. "Be back soon."

She grabbed her bag, stopping in the bathroom to check her appearance. Jeans, a white long-sleeved shirt and a hot pink vest. Lip-gloss and some mascara on her face. She looked decent enough. Except for her giant mop of crazy, curly hair.

She fished an elastic from her bag and twisted her hair into a messy pile on top of her head. Good thing Kim had hired a stylist to do the bridal party's hair tomorrow. No matter how many fashion magazines Jamie read, she'd never found an easy way to tame her long brown spirals. It was impossible. Not unless she spent hours on it.

But her appearance didn't matter to Dean, did it?

Outside, the midday sun was bright in the sky, but unpleasantly cool air was pushing off the Atlantic, a competition that would soon be won by fall's advance. Jamie grimaced. It was so depressing here when autumn came, the tourists gone, the shores quiet and empty.

It always reminded her of being left behind.

Something had pulled her home though, her feet sunk deep within the sands of Portland, the undertow dragging her back here like gravity. Not that she'd had another choice once competitive swimming was ruled out.

Midway through college, it became clear she'd reached her highest potential. No matter how brutal her training schedule—mandatory two-and-a-half-hour practices every weekday evening, additional ones at dawn three days a week—she couldn't earn a place in her NCAA division championships. Her speed had maxed out, her open turns on flat walls as good as they were going to get. And no matter how disciplined she tried to be, she couldn't keep up with the high-protein, low-carb diet of a professional swimmer. Having to watch what she ate was a Herculean task, especially when French fries beckoned a lot more than veggies, lean meat and fruit.

Her stomach grumbled in agreement. The lunch of roughage and tomatoes hadn't exactly satisfied her.

Jamie hurried to her car and checked the time. Dean was going to either say yes or no, and rushing over there wasn't going to change his answer. She had time to grab a bite.

Procrastination worked almost as well as dodging people.

She put her car in drive, blasting the radio as loud as she could. It did make sense for her to take the job her boss had offered, even if it meant accepting that coaching was going to be her full-time gig. She could love fashion all she wanted, but that world wasn't for her. It was intense and cutthroat and impossible to break in to. She didn't have the training, or the confidence. Not after those rejections had shown up at her door.

Jamie pulled into a drive-thru and waited, letting her head fall back against the seat. The career still beckoned. She longed to travel to places like New York, London, Milan and Paris. To spend her time around organza and tulle instead of spandex and terrycloth.

Fashion was the polar opposite of swimming, and maybe that had always been its appeal. There was so much freedom in the expression of creativity, and clothing held the power to elevate. One change of wardrobe, and you could go from being ordinary into a fairy-tale princess. From demure to provocative. Sweet to fearless.

Jamie wanted to do that—to create the kinds of clothes that made women feel strong and beautiful.

She knew she could've tried harder to get to New York. She could've applied to an unpaid internship and worked round the clock until she'd climbed her way up to being someone's assistant, but those jobs required writing and communication skills she didn't have. It also would've meant telling her parents what she wanted to do.

The idea of even mentioning it to them made her start to hyperventilate.

Designing clothes seemed kind of silly in a house full of doctors. Saying it was her dream would make her sound even more like the flighty person they thought she was. The one who never grew up, who was never serious about anything.

She'd gotten serious again, once. Enough to look up local programs and see if there was anything she could do. The Maine College of Art had a new program—a B.F.A. in textile and fashion design. A lot of it focused more on fabrics than drawing though, and Jamie had never gotten along with a needle and thread. Every project she'd made in Family and Consumer Science class had been a disaster and a half, and she'd practically cut her finger off the last time she used a sewing machine.

Besides, going back to school required money, and asking her parents to support her was not happening. Sure, they'd put the boys through medical school, but that was different. They were following in their father's footsteps, and success in their field was nearly a sure thing. There was no guarantee Jamie would ever make it big. She could take out student loans instead, but what were the odds she'd ever be able to repay them? She'd be in debt forever, while her brothers were making money hand over fist and chuckling over their crazy kid sister during their golf games.

All that aside, the possibility of getting rejected again was enough to ward her off from looking into the application. It had been a hard blow to her ego the first time. She didn't feel like getting crushed by it again.

She didn't want to think about that anymore. What she *did* have to think about was Dean, and how she was going to handle this whole situation.

The key was in acting like nothing had happened. To pass it

off the way she had back in high school, even though she'd wanted nothing more last night than to close her eyes and put herself in his hands, letting him play her body until her release became as inevitable as the tide.

Jamie shuddered. God, even the recollection of his touch lit her up like a torch. Maybe that was why, no matter how many guys she'd thrown between herself and that night, she couldn't shake Dean off.

It was hard to forget the best she'd ever had.

She had to, though. Her head was on board with the whole "just friends" thing, so her body would eventually fall in line too. For now she needed to focus on coming through for her family. It would be nice if she could do something to save the day for once, instead of being perceived as the single Matthews child who was silly and useless.

Jamie rolled ahead in line and ordered something greasy, telling herself she'd work it off in the pool on Monday. She munched on her food in the parking lot and geared herself up, rehearsing her practiced façade. She'd forced her way past awkwardness like this with Dean before.

She could do it again.

FIVE

Dean climbed into his truck and rummaged through the glove box for his external phone battery charger. The shiny device was this year's impersonal birthday present from his mother, but a useful one at that, considering how often he ran his phone down to nothing. It had taken him fifteen minutes to find it this morning, dead in the back pocket of his waterlogged jeans.

He let it charge and started up the engine, idling for a few minutes as he stared out at the harbor.

Ice-blue water hugged the land, the last few boats of the season remaining stubborn in their slips. October had just begun, and already the midday light had changed to something more orange than gold. The abundant green of Maine's oaks and maples was giving way to the fiery colors of autumn, little pops of color peeking out where leaves met the halo of blue overhead.

It was exactly the kind of day he would've gone out to photograph, back when he did that kind of useless shit.

The charger quickly powered up his phone, and Dean thumbed through his messages. He was almost glad the stupid thing had no juice all night long, because it was blowing up with texts now. One from the girl he met at the bar by Southern Maine Community College on Wednesday, asking what he was doing tonight. Another from the chick who'd sold him his coffee at the joint on the corner last week, her name and number scrawled on the side of the cup. Two more he couldn't differentiate between because they had the same damn name. Connor asking if he'd be checking out the cars at the county fair with him today. His father asking where the hell he was.

Dean rubbed his eyes and sighed. He'd slept in later than he planned, thanks to last night's fantastic decision making. It had been a frequent habit lately. He often liked to say that slacking on the weekends was one of the perks of working for his father. The truth was, he dreaded going there.

But it was past noon now. Time to get back to the grind.

Ignoring the other texts, he replied to Connor that he wasn't going to make it and kicked his truck into gear. Disappointment had him obeying the speed limit for once, driving more slowly than he should have, considering the time.

The car show at the local harvest festival was like being at the Bunny Ranch, with so much beauty everywhere Dean never knew what to look at first. Car enthusiasts came from miles around, showing off the kinds of 1960s muscle cars that had always been his favorite. Their sleek lines and pure machine strength embodied a feeling of danger and rebellion unmatched by any other vehicle. Finding the source of that power was what captivated him the first time his dad popped a hood and showed him all the metal, tubes and wires inside.

Dean always hoped he'd have a car to bring there, one to sit proudly next to with a beer in his hand, but that future was getting more and more dim every day. He couldn't even afford to get his own ride up to snuff. His '71 Chevy C10 pick-up worked well enough, but it wasn't anywhere near show condition. The bumpers needed some serious chrome, his engine wasn't pretty and the truck box he'd needed to mount to the bed in order to lug supplies around for the business had scuffed the hell out of the railings. It was an A-to-B vehicle, not a trophy piece.

Skipping the fair was just as well.

He decided against his usual coffee, half because of how late he was and half to avoid an uncomfortable conversation with the chick he'd met there. One date and she already wanted more than he was willing to give, calling him baby, stroking his tattoos and asking where she could get one like it.

The ink was where it always started. Women were drawn to the bad boy image that being covered with tattoos symbolized. It was part of the reason he kept going under the needle for more.

The other part—well, they didn't need to know about that.

His tats were personal reminders drawn into his skin, but Dean had woven a web of fiction around them, the kind of stories women liked to hear. Ones about power, strength and independence.

They'd follow him home like he was the Pied fucking Piper.

He'd be a liar if he said he didn't do it for the sex. His craving for it was easily proved by the rotation of women in and out of his bed. But reading them right was what turned his crank. He loved puzzling out what made them blush, what got their pupils to dilate or their nipples pebbling underneath their shirts. Finding their quirks, then doing whatever it took to make them explode.

Jamie had gone off like a nuclear bomb.

Dean groaned, his dick already responding to the faintest hint of the memory. Hers was the first reaction he'd gotten hooked on. The first sights, sounds and smells of a woman's pleasure that had turned him into a junkie for it.

The kink had served him well.

The problem was that each woman he brought home woke up the next morning wanting an all-access, unlimited pass to his apartment and a promise of commitment, which ended with him doing his best to let them down gently. It wasn't that he didn't care. He just knew the whole kids, dog and white picket fence thing wasn't for him, so it was better to end things before they got attached.

Another reminder to get these thoughts about Jamie the hell out of his head.

Ten minutes later he arrived at the rundown building that housed Trescott Auto Body. Dean grimaced as he pulled into the lot. The whole exterior needed a paint job, and don't even get him started on the roof. Fixing it wasn't essential yet, and they had to cut as many corners as they could. It had been hard to stay afloat ever since the big chain stores moved in. Dean guessed that was why his dad had filled up the warehouse with so much crap —he wouldn't let go of a single piece of junk in case it became useful someday.

None of it ever did.

They'd done better since Connor built them a website a few years back, but it still felt like a sinking ship, even when they could boast of employing some of the best mechanics in the area. Customers were more interested in saving a buck than going to experts who actually loved cars.

Then again, loving cars wasn't part of Dean's job. He oversaw the labor, made sure the right parts got delivered and kept everyone in line.

Assistant managers and future owners didn't have the luxury of loving things.

He pushed through the employees-only entrance and made his way across the floor to the door with a shiny gold sticker, the word "Management" stamped out in black. Chuck Trescott looked up from his desk when Dean stepped inside.

"Look who finally showed," he said.

With deep creases around his eyes and what was left of his hair gone almost completely silver, Chuck was a preview of what

Dean could expect to look like in twenty years, except worse and probably with a different set of worries packed onto his shoulders.

"Sorry." Dean flopped onto a chair that had seen better days and glanced at the pile of bills on his father's desk. "What's on tap for today?"

"Got some work orders for you to write up. A few inspections on a couple of wrecks too. Give me the lowest estimate you can."

Dean stifled a frustrated sigh. It didn't matter how much they low-balled the numbers. The insurance companies were the ones telling the clients where to go.

"You know we can't compete that way, Dad," he said quietly.

The comment went without an answer.

"Taking out the claims adjusters will bring in more customers," he added. "A lunch once a month, or even sending a basket of chocolates, and we'll be on the reps' preferred lists."

A gray eyebrow of warning was raised in Dean's direction. "We didn't have to wine and dine anyone to get work in your grandfather's day, and we're not doing it now."

No reply was necessary. Dean had tried to fight this battle before.

He escaped his father's glare and studied the photo of his grandfather on the wall. Sepia, faded at the edges, in an old wooden frame. He was standing in front of the building they were sitting in, back when it was new.

He looked happier than Dean had ever been here.

Fifty years ago, his grandfather had founded the shop on the idea of dealing fairly and honestly with their customers. Of creating real person-to-person connections, building relationships that lasted. It was why Dad refused to play the game with the insurance companies, insisting it was unethical to cut costs in exchange for steady work. But without the claims reps sending clients to their door, they had nothing setting them apart, other than the family name. They were barely even computerized.

"Hey, did you look into that virtual assistant bookkeeper I found?" Dean asked. "She was pretty reasonable. Ten bucks an hour."

"I didn't have time."

The "time" line was bullshit Dean had heard before. Dad was resistant to new technology, from search engine optimization on the website to software that would help with tasks and organization. Even convincing his old man to move the management system from a list he kept in his head to a whiteboard on the shop floor had taken a shitload of effort.

The entire situation was getting exhausting.

"We did get a possible new customer," his father said. "A guy called about a '71 Plymouth Barracuda he's acquired. The front end needs a rebuild but he wants vintage parts."

A small flare of excitement pitched in Dean's belly.

"We offering classic car restoration now?"

Normally they only fixed up modern vehicles after collisions. Taking on jobs like this—real high-end customization on the kinds of cars he loved—was part of what Dean had hoped for when he signed his life over to his father.

"Don't count on it. I'm only taking this job if we can make a profit." He handed Dean a sheet of paper. "Here's a list of everything we need. Get the best price you can. There's a wrecking service in New Hampshire that might have it all, if you don't have any luck locally."

Anticipation that Dean never should've felt in the first place sputtered out of him like a fizzling spark plug. This wasn't about the two of them, or loving cars at all. This was Dean being sent on a mission to hunt down the lowest price.

Resentment pressed at his sternum, a fire that wouldn't take much air to feed. Dean gritted his teeth and stared at the floor, words he wanted to say like a tornado in his head.

I don't want to keep doing this.

There's got to be a better way.

He kept his mouth shut. They'd been down this road before: Dean made suggestions, his father ignored them. And he knew his place here. He might've been third generation Trescott, but he was a grunt man, a cog in a wheel, trying to follow through with the vision his grandfather had.

It was fine. The salvage yard wasn't far from a seasonal antique car show he'd always wanted to hit. Maybe he could get Connor to go with him. Make a road trip out of it.

He took the list from his father's hand. "Anything else?"

"That doesn't sound like enough for half a day's work?"

"It is. Just want to make sure I've got it all covered. I'll get started."

Dean launched himself out of the chair. Two steps later, he had his hand on the knob and was out the door. It didn't matter that his father never listened. That was the status quo, and he needed to focus on work, to get jobs done and bring in more cash. He had no marketable skills other than this, so if the garage went down the tubes, he was going to be well and truly fucked.

Out on the floor, Dean paged through the work orders and tried to lose himself in the sounds and smells of the garage. The hum of the air compressor, the sharp grind of the sander and snap of the paint gun. The tangy mix of gear oil, leather cleaner and sawdust. He'd grown up around them and could identify each one with his eyes closed.

They made up his past, as well as his entire future.

Dean shook his head and exhaled heavily. He didn't know what he was complaining about. He had everything he needed in life. A roof over his head. Food on the table. Wheels to get around. Sex when he wanted it. Friends. Family. If he could only ignore this nagging part inside him that said he wanted *more*, that would be great.

The bell at the front desk rang out with a high-pitched ding. Dean glanced over through the Plexiglas window.

Jamie.

Oxygen was suddenly hard to come by. Shit, last night must've really upset her, otherwise why would she be here?

Dread settled like a dead weight in his stomach as he crossed to the door and opened it warily.

"Hey," he said. "Everything okay?"

Jamie heaved a dramatic sigh and parked her elbows on the desk. "I came to say goodbye. I'm pulling up stakes and heading out of town for good."

Dean's heartbeat stuttered. He blinked. Several times. "You are?"

"Gotchya." Her face broke out into her signature grin. "It was a joke, dumbass."

He huffed out a laugh, the sudden relief palpable. "Nice."

She stood up and slipped her hands in the pockets of a puffy vest. She looked good. Adorable actually, but it didn't seem like she'd dressed up for him, those crazy curls of hers wound up in a bun on top of her head. Nothing about her said upset at all. She was playing jokes, smiling, acting the same way she always did.

It was a good thing. He knew that. But something about her easy demeanor nagged at him, buzzing around his head like a mosquito in August.

"So what can I do for you?" he asked.

"I need your help with something."

Definitely not here about last night then. "Okay, shoot."

"The photographer for Sean's wedding got into a car accident. He's on his way to surgery and there's no backup, so we're totally screwed. I know you said taking pictures wasn't your thing anymore, but I don't suppose there's any way you could fill in?"

"Aw, Jamie, I don't know."

He wasn't sure if it was her request or the fact that she was acting so *normal* that was bothering him.

"Please," she said, barreling through his reluctance. "If you don't come, the only photos we'll have will be whatever the guests take on their phones." She paused, adding, "We'd pay you for your time and everything."

"I can't take money from you."

Money was a key factor in the separation of their worlds. She lived in a Victorian house on the shore. He lived in a warehouse. Dinners with his dad were pizza deliveries at the shop, while the Matthews were longtime members of the Portland Country Club. If he wanted to keep their relationship on an even keel, he couldn't let her pay him for something like this.

"Okay, then. No money." Her lips twisted to the side in an expression she often made. One that was weird and cute and made him want to kiss them back into place.

Stop it.

"What if I said there was free beer and food in it for you?"

Dean laughed loudly. Man, she knew him well.

"All right." He dragged the words out, trying to sound a lot more unenthusiastic than he felt. "I'm in. What time?"

She gave him the details and strode toward the exit in a flourish.

"Jamie, wait." It was too odd, the way everything had been so easily swept to the side. He couldn't let her leave without checking. "About last night..."

She waved a hand in the air. "It's no big deal. Forget about it."

Well, okay then.

He watched her leave, wondering what the hell he'd agreed to. He didn't have any experience photographing weddings. Hell, he didn't even know if his camera still worked. But he'd been compelled to say yes. To do something that made her happy.

He liked being the reason for her smile. It was probably why jealousy had snapped through him like a firecracker when she moved on in high school, a friendly wave thrown in his direction from the arm of the jock she went out with next.

It was a dumb feeling to have. He'd wanted her to find someone else. It was why he'd cut things off.

Dean retreated into the garage, finally able to get a grasp on what had been bugging him. He'd been looking for *something* with her—a hint of emotion in her eyes, proof that last night had some kind of effect. But his reality today was the same as it was six years ago, and she didn't belong here. One day she wouldn't be kidding about moving on, and he'd be happy for it. Her behavior was exactly what he should've hoped for.

So why did it feel like a pry bar was being jammed into his gut?

He shook it off. Helping her out was the right thing to do. To set things right and act like a real friend, for once.

It was the only way he could be sure her smile wouldn't become tainted for good.

SIX

Dean was enjoying himself a lot more than he'd expected.

The reception passed in a flurry of laughter, music and good food, although he hadn't had any of the free beers Jamie promised him. He'd been a bit rusty with his camera and wanted to stay sharp. Putting on the suit he hadn't touched in a while was another good reminder to lay off the booze. It fit, and he wanted it to stay that way.

He checked through the images on his camera, pretty happy with what he'd captured so far. The backdrop of cobalt blue ocean at the ceremony site. The bride and groom recessing down the aisle, guests raining a shower of fiery blossoms over them. The first dance, then Jamie's brothers holding up their beers as they sang along to "Sweet Caroline". Krissy and Mikey swaying to a slow song, a foot of space between them.

He hoped Mikey would remember some of the advice he'd given him and actually score tonight, but watching them together was like something out of junior high school. Except worse. And more awkward.

And then there was Jamie.

Dean sought her out in the crowded ballroom, locating her in the middle of the dance floor. She was laughing loudly, her head thrown back like she was on a roller coaster. She'd downed a couple of beers and more than her fair share of champagne, but what the hell. It was a party. And Jamie having fun was always a sight to be seen.

Not to mention her body in that dress. Jesus.

Short. Tight. A dark blue color that set off her skin perfectly, and fuck if it didn't highlight the tight circle of her waist and those badass arms. He'd wanted to find a corner to hide her in and see how good that dress looked in a puddle around her feet.

Dean beat back the fantasy when the staff rolled out the wedding cake. His camera battery didn't have much juice left and he didn't have a spare, so he quickly began snapping shots of Kim and Sean as they cut the first slice. Jamie was standing off to the side, and without realizing it, Dean suddenly found himself zeroing in on her. Her hair was straighter today, more wavy than curly. He liked it, but didn't think it suited her. He'd always seen her as too wild to be tamed, too fun to be trapped by any one style or life.

The last shot he got before the camera shut down was of her profile, the bride and groom blurred and out-of-focus behind her.

Discomfort landed like a sudden sucker punch. Dean pressed his hand to his belly, then loosened his tie. He was probably hungry or dehydrated. He hadn't eaten a thing all day, too busy making sure he did his job.

Moving to where he'd stashed his things in the corner of the room, he packed the camera away and took off his tie, leaving it in one of the camera bag's pockets. The bartender had saved him plate of food, which Dean tucked into and ordered a beer. He was off the clock now, so at least one free drink was in order before the night ended. He wolfed down his dinner and was halfway through a bottle of Shipyard Ale when someone tapped on his shoulder.

He glanced up. Jamie was behind him.

"Finished?" she asked.

"Yeah. Ran out of battery. Sorry."

"Don't be sorry. It's a lot more than we would've had without you." She reached a hand out. "Since you're done, let's dance."

She waited patiently, her cheeks rosy. Dean shook his head.

"I'm not a *dance at weddings* type of guy."

Jamie rolled her eyes and grabbed his hand anyway. "Whatever. It's the last song. You're dancing."

Dean had no choice but to abandon his drink as she towed him behind her. It was almost embarrassing how easily she pulled him where she wanted.

Not that he was protesting all that hard.

The words "Kick it" came out over the speakers, and then the band broke out in a rendition of "Fight for Your Right to Party". It was a shocker to hear a Beastie Boys song at such a posh place, but the bride and groom must have requested it, because they immediately rushed the floor.

Jamie released his hand and started to dance, but Dean held back around the periphery, doing some lame-ass bopping of his head and feeling like he didn't belong. But then she threw her hands above her head at the chorus, her fingers in devil's horns, and Dean couldn't help but laugh. It was amazing how easily she was able to let go, to have so much fun in everything.

He gave in. Throwing a fist in the air, he jumped to the beat and sang along, calling out the lyrics he remembered until his throat went hoarse.

It was the most fun he'd had in a long time.

She fell against him at the end, sweat on her brow. He thought the alcohol had finally gotten to her until she went up on her tiptoes and whispered, "There's something I want to do. Come with me."

The look on her face proved she was about to do something devious, and Dean wanted to stay wrapped up in the moment. To ride the wake of the rush she always seemed to be flying on.

She led him out of the ballroom. The rest of the club was empty. The private bar on the far end that would usually host evening cocktails was dark, the whole place rented out for them.

Amazing, how fantastic life was when you had money.

Jamie stopped by the entrance. The wedding gifts were stacked up on a table near it.

"Grab as many as you can carry," she commanded.

Dean was too worked up to argue. It had been years since he'd pulled any kind of prank, and it was impossible to resist her sly grin. They scooped up the lot in three trips, piling them into the backseat of Jamie's father's car. He didn't even know when she'd swiped the keys. Cackling as she reached the doorway, she paused to catch her breath and laid a hand on his chest.

"Okay, now look really upset."

Her energy was infectious. "Like this?"

Dean frowned, and Jamie snorted. "Not like someone just told you Santa Claus isn't real. Like something went horribly wrong."

He practiced an expression of utter horror. Jamie scrunched up her nose and shrugged.

"It'll do."

Inside, she strode straight up to Kim and Sean. Jamie tugged on Sean's sleeve.

"I've got to talk to you. It's important."

Sean's eyes went wide as he took in Jamie's solemn expression. The urgency in her voice nearly made Dean believe something awful had happened too.

"What is it?" Kim asked.

"It's the gifts. I don't know how, but someone must've put them on a golf cart, maybe to get them out of the way, I don't know. Anyway, I went outside to move them into Dad's car, and I think the cart got turned on accidentally because it's barreling toward the water and I can't stop it!"

Sean's mouth dropped open. "Are you shitting me?"

Laughter bubbled up inside him. Dean coughed into his fist to hide it. How did she do this with a straight face?

Jamie pointed her fingers at both of them, like she was firing off pistols. "Gotchya!"

Kim immediately started laughing. Jamie's brother, however, looked like he was about to throttle her.

"You promised—"

"I promised no pranks until *after* you were married. It's after, so all bets are off, suckers."

Sean clenched his hands into fists. Jamie came around behind Dean, hooked her chin over his shoulder and said, "Um...run."

They took off together, sprinting out of the ballroom and toward the vacant bar. They crashed through a set of French doors, stopping when they reached the far end of the room.

Dean whirled around. Sean hadn't followed them. He wasn't afraid of Jamie's brother, but he didn't want to have to take the guy out at his own wedding either.

"I think we're safe," he said. Jamie was too busy laughing to hear him.

She fell into a rounded booth in the corner and swung her legs up onto the middle of the cushion, her hands on her stomach as if it hurt to laugh. Her dress had inched up her thighs, the fabric clinging to her hips.

Hunger clawed at Dean at the sight of her body sprawled out like that. With her legs up on the seat, her head tossed back and her smile wide, she looked so relaxed. So free. So Jamie. He stopped at the edge of the table and stared at her legs, wanting so goddamn badly to be trapped between them, to finally be buried inside her, to feel her heat and watch her mouth drop open in pleasure.

What was he thinking? She was his friend. His *friend*. When was he going to get that through his skull?

Jamie finally stopped laughing. She sighed and smiled. "That. Was. Awesome."

"Yeah, you're pretty damn funny when you want to be."

Another giggle fizzled out of her. She looked ridiculously pleased with herself.

"We should probably lay low for a few," she said. "Until the rage gets out of Sean's system."

"Why do you do it?" he asked. "The jokes on your brothers."

He'd always found her prankster nature amusing, but never understood why she did it.

She shrugged. "Someone's gotta take them down a peg or two. Make them feel less like the gods they think they are."

There was more she was covering up, something other than sibling rivalry, but he couldn't get a handle on what it was.

"Are you just gonna stand there?" She patted the spot next to her. "Sit."

She lowered her legs and scooted over so he could join her. Dean held himself still, tension like a live wire inside him. It was as if every bone, every fiber in his body was dragging him forward, a magnet being pulled toward true north.

It wasn't a good idea, not only because she'd been drinking. It was because he *felt* it again—that fuse that always simmered beneath the surface between them, waiting for a spark.

It was a dangerous feeling. Dean didn't know if he had the power to resist it.

He sat down anyway. Jamie turned to face him, one elbow balanced on top of the seat cushion, her hand propping up her head. The motion put the soft, full curve of her breast into full view.

Dean clenched his jaw and clasped his hands together on his lap.

"Thank you for helping out today," she said.

"No problem. I had fun." His mouth went dry. He swallowed. "Thank you for hiring me."

She grinned, her eyes drifting closed for a second, and Dean jumped at the chance to take her in. The rounded apples of her cheeks. Her neck and collarbones and the flat of her stomach. Her legs, curled up and pressed together beneath her.

He wondered if she still tasted the same.

"I didn't hire you, silly. I bribed you with food and beer, which I hope you enjoyed."

He didn't answer, too distracted when she turned to the side and toed off her heels, then got back into the same position. She'd moved closer to him while she did it, or maybe he'd been the one to move, he wasn't sure. All he knew was that he could feel the heat radiating off her, her body so close, all that gorgeous hair tumbling down over her shoulders.

He had to tighten his clasped fingers to the point of pain to stop himself from touching her. God, when had he started wanting her this badly?

His voice came out gritty when he said, "I had a good time anyway."

"I'm glad." Her eyes fell on his collar. "You look good in a suit."

Dean's pulse ratcheted up to full throttle. She brought a hand up to trace the edge of his neckline. Soft fingers stroked his neck.

He hissed in a breath. "Jamie."

It came out sounding like he was trying to stop her, like he realized what was about to happen and the mistake they were about to make all over again. A war raged between his head and his body, between the right thing to do and what he wanted, but Dean's ability to reason was hanging by a thread, and he couldn't make himself sure this was a mistake anymore.

She shook her head. "Don't talk." Pulling him to her, she whispered, "Just don't talk."

Then she was kissing him, her mouth open and hot and hungry. She nudged his hands apart and crawled onto his lap, the warm weight of her legs on either side of him. Dean lost the battle he'd been fighting, giving in to everything he'd been wanting.

Wanting until he was taking.

He grabbed her by the hips and settled her more firmly over his lap. She groaned, and the sound went straight down his spine. Dean thrust against her, one quick lift that had him hard in seconds. His breathing grew heavy, breaths panted out through his nose until he was lightheaded, but he'd be damned if he stopped kissing her even for a second. He could live without air if it meant he could slide his tongue along hers, teasing dips into her mouth that had her grinding down on him like she couldn't get enough.

He sure as hell knew he couldn't.

She came up for air first, pulling back and working his shirt buttons with shaky hands. Two of them open and she fisted his collar, ripping it to one side to graze her teeth along his neck.

"Christ, Jamie."

She nipped and sucked the spot where his neck met his shoulder—Jesus *fuck,* he couldn't believe she remembered he liked that. Dean bucked up on instinct, head rolling to the side to allow for more. Every time she bit down it sent ripples of pleasure from his throat to his dick.

Time to show her he still knew how to push her buttons too.

He yanked her hands from his chest and wrenched them

behind her. She didn't fight him, just whined and rocked a little harder over him.

Oh yes. There it was.

Her wrists were small enough to fit in one hand, so he skirted his other one up her back and drove his fingers into her hair, fisting tight. She gasped when he pulled her head back. Dean hummed, loving the intensity of her reaction.

"That's right," he murmured. "I remember what this does to you."

He tugged harder, and she moaned. "Dean...please."

"Please what?"

He'd make her say what she wanted. After all these years, she'd better damn well say it out loud.

"Please touch me."

He let go of her hair and her chin drooped forward, her eyes heavy-lidded with lust. Dean released her arms and pressed his thumb beneath her jaw, drawing her gaze up, forcing her to look at him.

"You sure?"

Jamie nodded, a rapid movement he didn't want to question. She ground against him again, seeking more friction, surrounding him with heat. Fuck it all. She wanted him, and his brain was too foggy to figure this mess out anyway, to wonder what it would mean in the morning.

He carefully drew up the bottom of her dress, hiking it over her hips, then inched his fingers down until they met satin and lace. God, she was still his fucking wet dream, all soft skin and muscular thighs. She whimpered when he lingered there, her hips shifting toward his touch. It was a heady feeling, making her wait, and he kept doing it until she let out a thin cry of desperation. Palms framing her thighs, he urged her onto her knees. Jamie balanced her hands on his shoulders, and Dean checked her face one more time before slipping his hand into her panties and tracing a wet circle over her clit.

She panted out a curse, hands fisting in his shirt. He watched her movements, the way she rocked forward when he did something she liked. How she gasped when he rubbed someplace sensitive, how her mouth fell open when he got the rhythm right. She cried out in disappointment when he stopped, but her protests died quickly on a high-pitched mewl when he dipped lower and slid a finger inside her.

Hot. Tight. So fucking wet.

His cock throbbed at the feel of her slick clasp, but Dean ignored it, enjoying the view of her writhing above him as he pushed in and out in leisurely strokes. He added another finger, twisting, pressing along her front wall until she let out a deep moan. Wetness spilled over his hand.

"Dean...oh, *fuck*."

The surge of victory made him smirk, and he stroked her sweet spot again. She jerked above him.

"Holy shit, how are you doing that?"

Dean chuckled. "Shhh. Just feel."

Her forehead dropped against his, her eyes shut tight, breath on his face. He kept at it until her thighs began to tremble, but she wasn't there yet. He skimmed his free hand up her side, smoothing over her breast to thumb the stiff tip of her nipple. She jolted, her body spasming around the slow pulse of his fingers. Tugging her dress and bra down an inch, Dean nuzzled her breast and looked up her.

"Ride my fingers, Jamie."

She groaned, but didn't do it. Just opened her eyes again and stared at him as the quaking in her thighs moved up her body. Her arms were starting to shake. He knew she needed more to get there, but the way they were sitting wouldn't let him get the angle of his hand any deeper, and he wasn't going to do a damn thing to stop where they were headed, not even to change position.

"Come on, honey. Do it. I know what you need. I'll make it good for you."

He closed his mouth around her nipple and sucked. Jamie's head fell back again on a soft moan, and another splash of wetness drenched his palm. Finally she started to work herself over him, hips grinding, her hands clenched even more tightly at his shoulders. He tongued and stroked until her breathing changed, pants turning into abrupt little shudders.

He remembered that sound.

Scooting down slightly but never stopping the pumping motion of his hand, Dean brought his other thumb to meet it, coating the pad and running it over her clit. He knew right away when he found the right combination—it was like a gunshot, the way one touch made her go rigid and then start to thrash—and rubbed her soft flesh with quick circles, murmuring, "That's it, honey, there you go," until she finally cried out, shattering above him.

It was the most goddamn beautiful thing he'd ever seen.

Her face contorted in a mask of pleasure, she chanted his name like she couldn't believe it was happening, too good to be real. He felt the same way, dizzy with the sight of her coming again, knowing he was the one who got her there.

Dean watched her absorb every shiver until she slumped down, her face against his neck, her breathing fast. He slid his fingers free and brought his hand to his mouth.

Light. Sweet. The tiniest bit salty. Just like he remembered.

"God, Jamie. Come home with me." He had to grit his teeth he was so hard. He needed more. More of this. More of her.

She hadn't heard him, though. She pawed at his chest, clumsy hands slinking lower to unbutton his fly. He was nearly deranged for her touch, but he didn't want to keep going like this.

Not hidden in the back of a bar, worrying someone could walk in at any second. He wanted to take her to his bed, spread her out and drink in every glorious inch.

She managed to lower his zipper. He caught her hands in his.

Jamie lifted her head, her eyebrows hunched down low. "What's wrong?"

"Come home with me," he repeated, not wanting to have to figure out the why or the how or what was going to happen tomorrow. "We don't have to...it doesn't have to be a big thing. We can...just for tonight. *Fuck*." He hooked his arms over her shoulders and pulled her down onto him, so she could feel how crazy she'd made him. "Come. Home. With me."

She stared at him, teeth digging into a plump lower lip.

"Is that a good idea?" she asked. "I don't know. I'm not thinking clearly right now." She swayed a little, then giggled. "But I guess neither of us is, right? I mean, we've been drinking. This is what we do when we're drunk."

All the blood that had drained from his brain rushed back into it again. He thought she'd been sober enough to make this decision, but he'd read her all wrong, too eager to take what she was offering. She had no idea he hadn't had anywhere near as much to drink as she had, or the fact that unlike at the beach, he'd had no desire to stop.

And now they'd gone and made a mess of things. Again.

"I'm not drunk, Jamie."

"What?" A deep line dug itself between her eyes. "But I saw you. At the bar."

"That was my first beer. And I'd just started it."

She gaped at him, obviously confused. Dean sighed, his hard-on quickly subsiding. Damn it, why couldn't he stop fucking up when it came to her?

One of them had to start thinking clearly.

"You're right," he said softly. "It's not a good idea. I got carried away."

He re-buttoned his pants and shirt, then patted her hip. She shifted off his lap, wobbly like a fawn, and he helped her up as he stood. He took a minute to comb her hair through with his fingers, straightening out a few tangles he'd caused, then swept his thumbs over her cheeks, wiping away any traces of what had happened. Making sure she was presentable.

"Sean's probably calmed down by now. You should go back inside before anyone wonders where you've gone."

"Okay." Her eyes were two big pools of chocolate brown. She looked so flustered, so lost. It made him want to hold her and comfort her, to kiss the crown of those now-ragged curls and promise her everything was going to be all right.

The only way it was going to be all right was if they stopped doing this. They had to. It was too fucking hard.

"I'm gonna head out," he said. "I'll let you know when the pictures are ready."

He left the room without another word. He'd broken his own rule, getting his emotions involved, making something out of nothing, wanting something he could never have. He knew better than that. He wasn't what Jamie needed, and never would be.

He wouldn't let this happen again.

SEVEN

Jamie leapt off the diving board and dove into the pool. Wednesdays were her longest day: preschoolers' group lessons in the morning, private lessons until her guarding station at two, then coaching the town rec swim team until six. She'd been in the pool for hours, but retreated to it when her shift ended anyway, hoping for the clarity she always found underwater.

But even with the world blocked out, her hearing muffled, gravity lessened and her movements fluid, all she could think about was Dean.

Today was the first time she'd heard from him since the wedding three days ago—an emotionless text to let her know the photos were ready. She'd replied with a quick *okay*, not sure what else to say. What were her options?

Thanks for helping out again. Oh, and by the way, can we talk about what the hell happened on Sunday?

The whole day was still a blur.

She'd plied herself with liquid courage, drinking a little more champagne than necessary during a toast in the country club's bridal suite with Kim and Krissy. With her hair different and wearing that dress, Jamie had wanted to feel sophisticated. Glamorous.

Like someone who had her shit together.

The prospect of seeming that way for two hundred of her parents' friends had Jamie downing a second glass even before they headed out to the ceremony site. She'd been dangerously close to tipsy by the time she saw Dean, waiting for them at the front door. Dressed in a crisp pewter suit and silver tie, he was clean-shaven, hair neat, tats hidden.

The boy cleaned up *good*.

She didn't necessarily like him all buttoned up, but the fact that he'd done it for her, that he'd unearthed his camera and shown up because she asked him to, made her feel all kinds of things she shouldn't have been feeling.

It had been part of what made her reach for more booze.

It was stupid, but it wasn't just him, either. She'd needed to escape the pressures of the party, from having to smile and face questions about her career. All she wanted was to throw off her cares and enjoy herself, to forget about how she'd done nothing but tread water during the last three years of her life, and have fun.

She ended up having a bit too much fun.

Jamie glided forward, covering the last few feet before somersaulting off the pool wall and propelling herself several yards into her lane. What happened in that dark corner with Dean wasn't all his fault. She'd been clear-headed enough to know she wanted him.

Kissing him felt essential. Like she'd die if she didn't.

And he'd proved once again that he knew how to play her body like no one else could. Her orgasm nearly tore her apart, waves of pleasure that swept over her with a ferocious intensity, and Dean had drawn it out, touching and whispering and encouraging until she was sure she'd never move again.

Then he'd said the words *just for tonight.* They'd been a shrill starting whistle, a knife cutting through the haze of lust and bringing everything into focus. One night with him was what she'd been aching for, but it had been hard enough for her to bounce back the last two times, and they hadn't even slept together. How much would it muddy the waters of an already murky friendship if they finally did it when they were drunk, crossing that line completely?

He hadn't been drunk, though. He'd been completely sober. And Jamie had no idea what to make of that.

Her chin broke the surface at the other end of the pool. So much for clearing her head.

She climbed out, ditched her cap and goggles and dried off. Tugging on her lifeguard sweatshirt, she went into the break room and started filling out her daily paperwork. She'd meant to do it on her break, but spent it in her boss's office instead, wolfing down her lunch as they discussed her future. She'd plastered a smile on when he brought up the assistant director position again, pretending that scheduling lessons and coming up with pool curriculum was something she was genuinely interested in.

She'd talked her way into a little more time to think about it.

Finished, Jamie hung up the clipboard and retreated to the pool deck. She began piling the kickboards in the storage closet, letting each one fall with a satisfying thwack.

It was nuts to turn down a job that was basically being handed to her. She was like a celebrity when it came to swimming here—her glory days as a champion meant that everyone who came within fifty yards of a pool knew who she was.

It was something she could *do* though, not something she loved. Not anymore, anyway. Sure, it was cool when she helped an infant learn how to float or ran the rec team through the speed drills that helped her break that record. But accepting this job meant accepting that she was never going to do anything amazing with her life.

She wanted to be someone important. To do something important. It was a possibility that only felt real when she dressed up. When she pretended to be someone else.

Maybe that was why she'd never been able to cut ties and leave Portland. Here she already was someone, even if all that someone did was swim. Coaching was easy, and Lord knew she'd always looked for the easy way out.

Crazy, silly Jamie. She was never serious about anything.

No one in her family had asked any questions when she'd gone back to the ballroom on Sunday, which wasn't a big surprise. At least now her home had emptied out. Sean and Kim had left for their honeymoon, Brendan and Owen went back home, and her parents had gone off on a little post-wedding getaway. Krissy was the only one who'd stayed behind an extra day, finally vacating the premises yesterday.

Jamie had driven her to the bus station before her shift. The girl's incessant stream of questions had reached the limits of her patience, especially when Krissy asked why she and Dean weren't together.

Jamie hadn't had nearly enough coffee to deal with that one. What was she supposed to say?

"There's nothing going on between us."

"We're just friends."

"I want him so badly I can hardly function when he's around."

She'd replied that it was complicated. That they'd gone there more than once, realized they shouldn't have, and it was stupid to go down that road again. She'd figured being completely honest would wipe out the chance of Krissy asking *another freaking question*.

What she'd gotten instead was a lecture, the girl going on for longer than Jamie's brain could handle about people acting how they thought they should rather than how they wanted to, afraid of the consequences, and that she and Dean should stop pretending they didn't want each other and get it over with already.

As if it was that easy.

She'd thanked Krissy for the advice and sent her on her way.

The psychoanalysis hadn't been necessary. Jamie had already thought about Dean's little theory, wondering what Maslow would've said about last weekend's fiasco.

Sex was a basic human need, so she'd probably earned herself a few hierarchical points with that. She'd only been following her physical instincts, trying to satisfy a craving. But still wanting Dean, when they'd proven several times it could never work out? Maslow probably would've said that ranked pretty high up there on the list of the dumbest things she'd ever done.

Dean Trescott was a bad habit, an addiction Jamie needed to kick. She needed to get herself unhooked, not dive headfirst into it.

Unless it *was* only for one night.

She stared at the kickboards, Dean's words like a dart to a bull's-eye. Maybe the reason she hadn't been able to drop this hunger for him was because they'd never technically done the deed. She needed to move on, but she couldn't do that until she got what she wanted.

Until she'd satisfied this need.

If they did it, then there was a chance she'd be able to get him out of her head. The idea of "just one night" had alerted her mental warning system when he'd said it, but if *she* was the one to suggest it, with every intention of walking away, maybe that would work. She didn't want to navigate their way back to friendship again after another drunken episode, but if they went into it with their eyes open, both of them knowing what was expected afterward, then maybe she could find the kill switch on this crazy cycle they had going and kick her craving for good.

Neither of them would be hoping for more. She wasn't any more capable of commitment than he was. Dean's attention span was limited, and she wasn't stupid enough to think she'd be the woman who changed him.

She didn't want to change him.

She *did* want to sleep with him, though.

Done for the day, Jamie showered and dressed quickly, blasting a hair dryer at her curls until heat and defrizzing serum beat them into spiraled submission. Her shoes made a clattering sound against the community center's floor as she hurried outside. She tugged her sweater closer and eyed the darkening sky with disdain. The sun had already sunk halfway past the horizon when a few months ago it would've been bright overhead. Jamie hated it, but wishing for year-round summer was pointless, and she drove toward the harbor, her grip tight on the steering wheel when she arrived at Dean's place.

His truck was in the lot. She made a point not to look at it.

She climbed the rickety outside stairs to his apartment, took a deep breath and put on her game face. Two short raps of her fist were followed by footsteps, but it was Mikey's face that peeked around the big steel door after it creaked open.

She knew he stayed here sometimes. Problems at home. He'd never shared the details, and Jamie didn't know him well enough to ask.

"Hey. Is Dean here?"

He nodded and let the door swing open.

Jamie walked past him and into the open space that was Dean's kitchen, living and dining rooms combined. It wasn't an inviting space. The windows lining the far end didn't have any coverings, and the light fixtures hanging from the ceiling were nothing more than bare bulbs.

But she was unable to focus on that, or anything else, once she saw Dean.

Black track pants were hanging low off his hips, arms running with sweat as he drew his chin up toward an exposed pipe. His shoulders trembled with the effort of lifting his body weight, voice strained as he grunted out numbers. His torso was bare, all his ink gloriously exposed.

Jamie's mind dissolved into a word that could only have sounded like *gnuh*.

Dean didn't notice her standing there though, too busy finishing his set.

"Fourteen...fifteen!" He dropped to the floor and laughed. "Told you I could do it, Mikey. Good thing the pizza's here because I win the bet. Dinner's on you."

He reached for a towel to wipe off his hands, then stopped when he saw her.

"Oh," he said. "Hey. You're not the pizza guy."

"Yeah. No."

His grin was lopsided. Something flashed in his eyes. Hope, maybe? "What's up?"

Jamie glanced over at Mikey, an awkward silence hovering like an ocean fog at dawn. He reached for his jacket. "I can leave—"

"No," she said, shaking her head. "I, uh...I came for the pictures."

It wasn't the truth, not entirely, but figuring out how to fuck one of your closest friends without it being weird wasn't a conversation for mixed company. She prayed Dean would somehow pick up on that.

He didn't.

The doors to the emotion she'd seen on his face closed up tight, rolling down like a castle gate and slamming shut.

"No problem," he said stiffly. "They're down in the truck."

He brushed past her, threw on a hoodie, zipped it up and snatched his keys. He opened the door and went downstairs without her.

Jamie lifted her chin and crossed the room to join him. "Later, Mikey."

He waved. When she reached the pavement, Dean had his hood all the way up, as if he were using it as extra protection, a cotton barrier between them.

"You working out now?" she asked the back of his head.

"Yup." He didn't look at her until he'd unlocked the truck box and handed her a plastic bag. A thick envelope was inside. "Here's the pictures."

Well, this wasn't going the way she'd planned.

It was getting cold. A front was pressing against the shore, the clouds dark and ominous, a warning they should listen to. Dean crossed his arms and leaned back against his truck. Distant. Standoffish. Jamie had half a mind to drive away, but she'd seen something in his eyes upstairs. She was sure of it. And she didn't want to leave things like this, either.

She looked down at her attire, trying to siphon strength from it. Black skinny jeans, gray sweater over a white tank, a set of shiny bangle bracelets and sparkly flats. The outfit screamed *I'm a girl who knows what she wants.*

She was, wasn't she?

She balanced a hand on her hip and popped it out to the side. "I'm thinking maybe you were right."

"About?"

"About us."

Dean made a sound that was a mixture of a laugh and a cough. "Okay. What was I right about?"

Jamie took a breath. "One night."

His eyebrows skyrocketed toward the tendrils of hair hanging down out of his hood. "One night..."

She gave him a look, a pursing of her lips that said stop playing around. "Six years of sexual tension. I think it's time we did something about it, or it's going to drive us both nuts."

Some of that anger melted off his face, the hint of a smile returning. He shoved his hood back and rubbed a palm over the back of his head. He'd gotten a haircut, something she'd missed before when she was too busy drooling over his body. The sides had been shorn to a soft buzz-cut she wanted to touch, to feel the baby-soft bristles on her fingertips.

His voice was low when he finally replied, "Is that what you want?"

Brilliant green eyes were trained on her, intense and sharp and overwhelming. The skin on Jamie's neck tingled with awareness.

Time to ante up.

"Yes," she said. "But just a night. To get it out of our systems."

Dean chuckled. "You think one night would get me out of your system?" He folded his arms again and smirked, his grin wolfish. "It would take a lot more than that, honey."

He was being the legendary Dean Trescott now, seductive powers out in full force. Jamie pushed past it, wanting to see her friend behind the pretty packaging.

The *very* pretty packaging. Guh.

"Yeah, yeah. You're great in bed. I know." She rolled her eyes. Smug bastard. "I'd only want to do it if I knew it wouldn't be a problem, like you said, and then go back to normal after."

It was empowering—finally putting it out there, saying what she wanted, especially with the caveat that she planned to put a stopper in things after she'd gotten it.

Dean stared at her, his gaze quiet and pensive. His sweatshirt was only partially zipped. His chest peeked out from beneath gray cotton.

He really was staggeringly handsome. Jamie's pulse pounded.

"I have to go out of town on Friday," he said. "New Hampshire. An errand for the business." He fixed his eyes on her lips, lingering there before trailing back up to her eyes. Jamie could feel the memory of his mouth on hers, the heat. Her tongue slicked over her top lip. "You could come with me."

She quirked up a brow. "Yeah?"

"Yeah. There's a car show out there I wanted to hit. I was going to drag Connor with me, but two nights in a hotel with you could be a lot more fun."

Desire shot through her like lightning, hot and needy. "A whole weekend, huh?"

He nodded. Slowly. "We get it out of our systems, then come back home and leave it all behind us."

A grin washed over her face. "What happens in New Hampshire stays in New Hampshire?"

He laughed. The husky sound put Jamie's entire body on lockdown, her breathing going fast and shallow.

"Exactly." Dean hooked one finger into each of her belt loops and pulled her against him. Their lower bodies collided. "Two days. Nothing held back. Everything we want. Just forty-eight hours of my hands in your hair and you stripped down to nothing."

Jamie's mouth dropped open in a sudden gasp. Her hips rolled without her permission.

His gaze flicked down to her waist. "That was pretty."

Her cheeks flushed. She ducked her face down. It was hard to keep eye contact under his white-hot scrutiny.

Dean wasn't having it. He brought one hand up, took a strand of her curls between two fingers and tugged on it twice.

Her eyes snapped to his, her body suddenly stretched tight like a too-taut rubber band. Dean smirked.

"I know what flips your switch, Jamie, and I'm going to trip it over and over again. I'm going to find all those spots I found years ago, and watch you shiver when I touch them. Kiss them. Lick them. I'm going to make you come so hard you forget your own goddamn name."

Jesus, *fuck*.

A shudder raced down her spine. Screw waiting for the weekend. She wanted to get started right now. She leaned in to kiss him, but Dean pulled back, holding a finger up.

"One rule," he said, his voice serious. "Nobody drinks. We stay sober the whole time, to make sure our heads are clear."

Smart move, one she'd thought of already too, but it still felt like a dig. She needed to get their equilibrium back. Jamie jutted her chin in the direction of his stomach.

"Fine with me. It'll help you get those couple of extra pounds off."

Dean laughed again and shook his head, the mood broken. "You ass."

She grinned back. This felt comfortable. Like *them*.

"You'll be able to get Friday off?" he asked. "I was planning to head out in the morning."

She shrugged. There was always someone at the center who needed to switch a shift. "It shouldn't be a problem."

"Good. And at home?" The question felt loaded, banked with subtext. "You want to tell them you're going to visit Gabriella or something?"

It would've been a good lie to use, if she'd needed it.

"Nobody at home to tell. My parents are away. And even if they weren't, I don't think it would matter much."

He frowned but didn't push it.

"Got it," he said.

Jamie inhaled, letting the reality of what they were about to embark on sink in. Two days until her fantasy finally became reality. She was charged up, eager. Hungry.

Ready.

"So," she said. "We good?"

Dean smiled—a knowing, suggestive one that sent adrenaline racing through her.

"We're good."

"Great. What time are you picking me up?"

EIGHT

Jamie finished packing, double-checked the house and locked it up before stepping out onto the porch. She'd sent her mother a text the day before saying she was going out of town on an impromptu trip with friends. She'd gotten the *Have fun,* response a little while later, a smiley face along with it.

Because emoticons could suffice where actual communication couldn't.

She left the envelope containing the photos from Sean's wedding on the kitchen table. She hadn't peeked inside, not needing the reminder of her eldest sibling's perfect life, even if Dean was the one who'd taken them.

She dropped her duffle on the porch and sat on the steps, waiting for his truck to appear. Her jacket formed a flimsy barrier against the October chill when all she had underneath it was a black turtleneck and jeans, but it was a worthy sacrifice in the name of fashion. She didn't understand what he needed to do today—something to do with poking through parts until he found several diamonds in the rough, so a sweater-dress didn't fit the bill. A pair of sturdy cowgirl boots she'd found at the outlets in

Kittery seemed appropriate, because finding anything decent on clearance surely had to be as difficult as whatever it was Dean was searching for.

The combination of denim and cowhide made her feel strong, confident. She hoped Dean would like it.

She hoped he'd like the rest of the clothes she'd packed too. Lingerie included.

They were staying at an inn off Lake Winnipesaukee. He'd let her pick the place, saying it was a business expense and he'd be able to write it off. She didn't want to spend too much, but she didn't want to get busy in some cruddy motor inn off the highway either. Bed bugs and sex were not an ideal combination.

Sex with Dean. Jamie stifled a grunt.

The prospect of what they'd be doing tonight was like a hit of adrenaline, her insides going suddenly molten at the thought of being trapped by those powerful arms, his attention solely on her. The blissful invasion of his body inside hers, without worrying about the mess it would make in the daylight afterward.

These fantasies would have to stop after the weekend, but that was fine. She'd only been harping over him because he was an itch she'd never scratched. In forty-eight hours that would be taken care of, and she'd be able to move on.

Her phone beeped. Jamie thumbed quickly over the screen. Dean's text was short and simple. *Be there in two.*

She stood, heaved her duffle over her shoulder and went down the front walk, nerves undulating in her belly like the pitch of red-flag waves. She stopped at the curb and looked at the sky when the call of a flock of birds rang out overhead. Jamie craned her head to follow their journey south until they slipped out of sight.

It used to depress her, watching the birds leave, but for the first time she didn't mind. Maybe it was because she was on her own voyage to someplace exciting, even if it was only for a few days.

Dean's truck rumbled down the block and came to a halt in front of her. He hopped out and flipped open the truck box. She tossed her things inside, pausing when she saw his camera bag at the bottom. Was that where he kept it, or had it been there since the wedding, an oversight he'd forgotten about?

Something to touch on later.

They climbed inside, and Dean grinned at her from behind the steering wheel. All at once she saw two versions of him: half the mischievous teenager she'd known as a kid, and half the grown-up playboy he'd become.

She was excited to be around both of them.

Two hours later they'd left I-95 for the winding county roads that would lead them to Lake Winnipesaukee. There hadn't been a rest stop in a while and the coffees they'd grabbed had gone right through her. Jamie gripped the door handle, grimacing as the truck bounced into the dirt lot for the salvage yard. She eyed a sign on the front door that said *The better-than-nothing restroom is around the back.*

"You brave enough?" he asked.

She wrinkled her nose. "I'm glad I wore my boots."

He chuckled and wished her luck. It wasn't as bad as she'd expected, and she made her way back out to the yard without incident. She surveyed the spread in front of her—one hundred acres filled with heaps of busted metal, some piled up on top of one another, cars with their interiors open, mechanical guts on display. She found Dean and started toward him, admiring how beautifully the shrugged-up sleeves of his black Henley shirt showcased his broad shoulders, his forearm corded as he bracketed a hand on the hood of something old and red.

"Find what you came for yet?" she asked.

"If it were that easy, do you think I would've scheduled the whole day for it?"

She leaned over the car and pushed her bottom out, taunting him with the suggestive curve of her rear. "Anything I can do to help?"

His eyes cut over to her, then away again. "Not like that, you can't."

Jamie stood up and stuck out her tongue. Dean reached out and squeezed her side, digging his fingers in until she squealed. She squirmed and batted his hand away, but he was too quick. He curled his fingers beneath her sweater, teasing her bare skin with two quick swipes before pulling them free. Jamie hissed in a breath, her nipples pebbling to sharp points.

"Somebody's impatient," he murmured.

She glared at him, but couldn't hide her smile. "Just find what you're looking for."

She followed him around the lot, watching as he picked through parts and talked to the owner, assessing classic pieces from the junk. It was nice, seeing him in his element, but boredom after an hour had her asking for his keys and waiting in the cab. Her boots thrown up over the dash, she listened to the radio and played aimlessly with her phone. Dean finally trudged out by the time she'd exhausted every diversion available, his eyes on the ground and one hand rubbing the back of his neck.

Jamie opened the door to greet him, not liking the look on his face at all.

"Bad news," he said. "They don't have what I need."

"So what does that mean?"

"It means I've got to cut this weekend short so I can keep looking. I'm sorry."

Her stomach bottomed out. She bolted upright on the seat and turned to face him. "Are you serious?"

He grinned full and wide. "Gotchya."

Jamie's mouth dropped open. She jabbed out a fist to punch him, but he darted back before she could make contact.

"You suck," she said, crossing her arms even as amusement and relief filled the void disappointment had created. Dean hung his arms on the roof of the car and leaned over her. The sun lit up the tips of his hair like a halo.

"Looks like somebody can't take what she dishes out."

Jamie glowered at him. "Shut up. You're mean."

Her ire was short-circuited when he ducked his head into the cab and bracketed her hips with his hands. He traced his lips from her cheek to her ear. Warm breath grazed her skin.

"Don't pout," he whispered.

His chin and jaw were covered with more scruff than usual, the bristles a soft, tickling scrape. Her arms fell open without her permission, hands dropping to curl around his wrists, legs parting and welcoming his body between them.

God, it was so easy for them to get like this. To go from friendly banter to *holy-shit-I-want-you* in two seconds flat.

Dean pulled back, gazing at her as he breathed in deep, like he was drinking in her reaction. Savoring it.

"I found what I need," he said. "I'm almost done."

She snaked a hand between them, fingers lifting the bottom edge of his shirt to chafe his stomach with her nails. He sucked in a breath and his shoulders jerked.

Payback was sweet.

"Good." She toyed with the button on his jeans. "Hurry up."

He snatched her hand away. "Behave."

The order sent a thrill through her.

Jamie pressed her clit against the seam on her jeans, a little bit of friction to stifle the ache. It was another half hour before he returned with the owner, pieces of metal being heaved onto the flatbed, tied down and covered with a tarp. The lunch hour was long gone by the time they were finally on the road again, and they grabbed sandwiches at a little lakeshore spot before cruising into Meredith Bay.

Dean parked while she checked them in, and met her in the lobby with both their bags easily slung up over his shoulder. They walked in silence down the hallway, and Jamie's heart thrummed wildly with the fact that this was real. They weren't stupidly intoxicated or swept up in the moment.

They both wanted this.

Inside the room, he dropped their bags to the floor and closed the curtains. Jamie stood by the bed, unable to move as he turned around and stalked closer. His movements were measured, purposeful, eyes holding her in place like a silent, cunning predator. Despite the fact that she was entirely covered up, the way he looked at her made Jamie feel as if she wasn't wearing anything at all. As if he could see through her clothes to the pearled tips of her nipples, to the panties that had become incredibly damp.

He backed her up to the wall and pressed her against it, trapping her hands in his and raising them both up over her head. Captured like that, Jamie expected hard and fast, but he leaned in slow instead, his lower lip making a gentle pass over hers.

A quiet moan escaped her.

He did it again, taking his time with soft brushing kisses. She tried to get closer to him, to deepen the contact, but he held her there with an unyielding grip, each unhurried kiss chased with a teasing slip of tongue. The combination of rough and sweet was like being caught in a heavy ocean current, buoyant and crushing.

Jamie's whimper was met with a low chuckle. Dean covered both her hands with one of his, nose skimming over her face to her neck as his free hand eased down her side. Spanned her waist. Slid between her thighs.

An opened-mouthed kiss to the tender spot beneath her jaw made her shudder. Dean hummed approvingly.

"I can't wait to taste you," he said. "To fuck you."

She whined, need coiling in her belly. Everything that had held her back from wanting this disappeared. Reality was days and miles away.

In this quiet room, there was only him. Only this.

"Please," she whispered.

"Not yet."

He pressed the heel of his palm along her pubic bone, then swept it up her body and grabbed a fistful of her hair. She gasped, a smile blooming as she gave in to the sensation, her limbs going liquid.

"First, you owe me."

The abrupt way he let her go was almost as rough as the growl in his voice. He stared her down, his own breathing labored as he whipped his belt to the side and yanked his jeans open.

"I owe you?"

Dean nodded. "For the wedding."

He grabbed the hem of her sweater and rucked it up over her head. She barely had time to orient herself before he was kissing her again, hands cupping her breasts, fingers strumming her nipples through her bra. He gave them a light pinch she could feel in her clit. Fuck, he really did know her triggers. Then he was grasping her wrists again, drawing them to his boxers and molding her hands over the stiff shape of his cock.

"Make me come, Jamie."

She bit her lip as she outlined him through the cotton. He was as big as she remembered, more thick than long, girth she'd barely been able to wrap her fingers all the way around. She glided her palm over the wet spot where the fabric pressed against his crown. Wanting to see the bare skin of his chest and finally get a glimpse of his ink up close, she tugged at the bottom of his shirt. Dean wrenched it over his torso and threw it to the side.

He was a piece of artwork in the flesh.

Jamie ran her hand over the length of his tribal sleeve, then down his side to where birds in flight spanned his rib cage. A compass rose was on his other shoulder, oddly missing their directional markings. Black stars were peppered like shrapnel over his heart.

When she looked up again, the playboy's smirk was gone. Anticipation radiated from every locked limb, eyes blazing as he watched her intently.

He liked watching her. Funny that she'd never noticed that before. That as much as she loved having his gaze focused on her, there was something he liked about it too. Something he craved. Needed.

She slid down to her knees.

"Fuck, yes," he said, bracing himself against the wall.

Jamie dipped her fingers past his waistband, pushing his boxers and jeans down to his ankles. It felt like Christmas when she found the prize waiting for her—hard, glistening at the tip, and all hers. She skated her hands up his legs, caressing his skin and the downy blond hair on his belly and thighs. She'd been waiting for this too long to rush it, but the way his cock jutted toward her suggested Dean wasn't interested in being teased.

She gripped the base with one hand and waited one last delicious second, looking up at the hunger in his eyes before closing hers and sucking the head into her mouth.

He groaned. Jamie smiled before taking him deeper, one long plunge that brought her lips to her fist.

"Jesus, Jamie," he whispered. "Goddamn."

She did it again, enjoying the heavy feel of him in her mouth and the sound of his panted breaths, then dipped her head to lick slowly up the underside of his shaft. A flick over the head. Hand lowering to cup and stroke his balls. A sharp hiss drew her gaze upward. Dean's eyes were fixed on her. His parted lips spoke volumes.

"Like that?" she asked.

He responded with a quick, silent nod. Jamie dragged her tongue along her palm and slicked it over him, pumping his rigid flesh until he moaned and his eyes fell shut.

God, it was such a rush. Such a fucking high to see him like that, weak with pleasure.

She went back to work, and it wasn't long until his hips were moving in time with her hand and mouth. A tremor ran through his legs as if he were holding back, wanting to plunge deeper but not letting himself.

She didn't want him polite. She wanted him unhinged. Frantic.

She drew back long enough to murmur, "Take what you want, Dean."

One whispered curse was all the warning she had before he dug his hands into her curls, fingers tightening into fists against her scalp. He held her in place as he set the pace, fucking her mouth. Jamie moaned in response around him, loving the feeling of being so brutally, unapologetically used.

"You like this," he choked out. "Show me how much."

She moaned again, and his next grunt broke on a shudder. His eyes drifted shut before snapping open again, like he was battling the urge to close them so he could keep watching.

He lost the fight.

His eyes slammed shut as he let out a hoarse groan, and Jamie welcomed the tang of his release. On her knees and immobile, she'd never felt more powerful, more wanted. She drew his orgasm out with deeper pulls of her lips and tongue, easing off when his grip in her hair loosened and his breath rushed out, gasping, spent.

She licked her lips and grinned up at him. "Have I sufficiently repaid you now?"

Dean peeled his eyes open, still short of breath. "For the moment."

He drew her up by her elbows and wrapped his arms around her. Surprisingly sweet kisses lingered and grew deeper as he palmed her waist, his thumbs skimming over her belly. Jamie squirmed.

"Something you want?" he asked between kisses.

"You might be satisfied, big boy, but I'm going nuts over here."

Dean's smile spread beneath their kiss, and then he was quietly unbuttoning her jeans, patient as he pulled the zipper down.

Jamie went up on her tiptoes when he dragged the fabric down her legs, stepping out of them as he kicked off his boots and shoved their clothes to the side. He was completely naked while she was still in her bra and panties, but he didn't seem in any way the vulnerable one, so big and burly and driving her crazy with his tongue. She lowered her hands to score his backside with her nails. He answered by making a leash out of her hair and snapping her head backward.

Jamie grunted, tiny shivers coursing through her.

"What is it about this?" he asked. "Why do you like it so much?"

She swayed slightly, sinking into the decadent pinch. "I don't know. Feels good."

"Hmmm." He bent his head to her breast and nipped at her nipple through the satin. "I think it's more than that."

"You're the Casanova," she replied. "You tell me."

He pressed himself fully against her, holding her between his body and the wall.

"I think it's not about having your hair pulled or your arms trapped. You don't want to just *come*. You want to be completely lost to the moment. A slave to it."

His free hand snuck beneath the waistline of her panties, glancing over her clit.

"You want to shut your mind off. To have someone else take charge. To be able to stop thinking and feel, and this—" He fisted tighter. "—helps get you there."

Jamie tried to absorb his words through the hazy fog of pleasure he'd put her in. Was that why it was always so good with him, why she felt so free when he took the reins? For years she'd craved being lost to it again, to be overcome by the rush. To feel wild, dangerous, and let loose that untamed part of her everyone else saw as the reason for her failure.

"I guess sometimes it's nice to be able to completely let go."

His brows shifted down low, but he didn't say anything. Stripping away the last of her clothes, Dean walked her to the bed. He kissed her again and pressed her down onto it, fingers weaving through hers, clasping their hands together and drawing them once more over her head.

"Hands on the headboard," he ordered softly. "Around the slats."

She did as she was told, hooking them onto the wooden poles. Dean stepped away, returning a moment later with a condom, and his belt.

Her eyes widened.

"To keep you still and help you let go." Dean knelt beside her and waited for her answer. "Yes?"

She paused, glancing at the belt, then back at him. She'd felt so liberated when it was Dean's hands holding her down. Nothing would help her let go as much as being fully restrained.

She wanted this. Fuck yes, she wanted this.

Jamie offered him her hands. "Yes."

He placed the condom on the nightstand, then carefully

wrapped the belt around her wrists and slid the leather through the buckle. She closed her eyes when he brought her bound hands back above her head, feeling the pull as he looped the belt through the rungs, tugging once to remove any slack.

The backs of his knuckles stroked over her cheek. Jamie opened her eyes.

"You can pull free pretty easy if you get scared," he said.

It felt snug enough. It was all the illusion she needed. "I trust you."

Something in his expression softened, and he climbed on top of her again, pressing kisses downward until he reached her belly. He grinned when he nipped at her there, eyes glittering with mischief. For a second, Jamie couldn't help wondering how many other girls he'd looked at like that. If that was the look that had made him a legend.

The thought vanished when he bent down and lapped at her clit.

Her hands lifted involuntarily, but the belt held her in place. She sank into the feeling, legs spreading wider, body twisting when he did something amazing with his tongue and tested how slick she was with the plunge of a single finger.

It was too much, too fast. She'd never come so quickly before, but he was a magician with his mouth. Gentle suction and flicks of his tongue combined with deep strokes over her G-spot drew her so swiftly to orgasm she barely had time to curse in surprise. Her back arched, the buckle jangling as she thrashed, body rolling with the force of all that pleasure. Dean helped her through it, his touch never ceasing until she collapsed against the blanket.

"Beautiful," he said. "You are fucking beautiful."

She smiled meekly, and he undid the belt. Her arms felt wobbly when he released her, but he was hard again and she wanted to touch. She wrapped her fingers around him, one slow pump before she squeezed. His eyelids drooped and he groaned.

"Condom?" she asked.

He panted through a smile. "You ready for more already?"

"I've been ready for six years."

Dean stared at her until panic flashed in her gut. The worry that she'd gone too far, said too much, was an anvil on her chest, but then he reached for the foil wrapper on the nightstand. Jamie swore his hands were shaking when he ripped it open and sheathed himself.

Kneeling between her open thighs, Dean paused as his cock nudged her pussy, as if he were about to say something. A reminder that this was sex, nothing more. She grabbed his hips and pulled, cutting him off, not wanting to ruin the moment with a good, hard dose of reality.

They both moaned when he sank inside her.

"Fuck," he ground out. "Jamie, *fuck*."

He let her acclimate to the exquisite burn, easy moves back and forth until one slick thrust made him go taut with tension, a switch flipped inside him. He lifted one of her knees, drew back to change the angle and slid home so deep that Jamie's hand slapped against the bed.

"Dean. God. Yes."

The words came out like she was choking. It wasn't just because of his size or skill, but because it was *him*, stretching her. Filling her. He surged again, and she reached for him with her other hand, wrapping her fingers around the back of his neck.

"Jamie." Her name was nothing more than a grunt. "God, you feel so good."

He wrapped her legs around him and started a rhythm, steadying himself with one arm braced against the mattress, the other fisting the blanket like it was already more than he could take. Jamie undulated beneath him, shocked by the rush of sensation. There was no way she could be about to come again, but it was there, pooling in her belly. Dean sped up, movements growing jerky. Jamie felt him tremble.

"Don't stop," she begged. "Please don't stop."

His eyes pressed tightly shut in a grimace of pleasure, he reached blindly for her hand and brought it between their slippery bodies. The first stroke of her fingertip over her clit found her sensitive and ready, and Dean dropped his forehead to meet hers, clutching the sheets with both hands.

"Holy shit," he gasped. "Jamie...I'm not, *fuck.*"

His restraint gave way, and something about it pushed her over the edge too. Dean leaned in, silencing her cries of pleasure with a kiss. His arms locked with one last hard shiver, and he fell against her, shuddering breaths hot against her neck until they both finally calmed.

He disposed of the condom, then rolled onto his back beside her. Jamie curled against his chest and closed her eyes. His fingers roamed through her hair, easy now, tender, and he pressed a kiss to her forehead.

Right before sleep claimed her, she had the fleeting thought that it might not be so easy to deal with this weekend ending after all.

NINE

Dean woke up Saturday morning to find Jamie sleeping soundly next to him. It didn't take long to remember pulling her to him the night before, when they'd collapsed in a sweaty heap after ordering room service, cracking up over some stupid TV show and having another hot-as-hell fuck session.

It didn't take long for his cock to realize they were both still bare-ass naked, either.

He ignored it, turning instead to look at her.

Early morning sunlight stole in through a crack in the curtains, bathing her in its rays. Her skin seemed even darker against the contrast of the rumpled white sheets. Her body was insane, from her toned arms to the two matching dimples at the small of her back, the perfectly flat expanse of her stomach and the delicate navel he hadn't been able to resist dipping his tongue into.

He'd felt like a super hero when he went down on her, practically drunk off the sounds of her pleasure. Last night blew him away, every second of it a dream come true. He'd imagined the hair-pulling thing was rooted in some kind of kinky vibe with her, a question that was answered when she talked about letting go. Dean wasn't one hundred percent on what that was all about, but he knew how to push her buttons, and bringing out the belt took it to the extreme.

God, her eyes. The way they'd widened, her cheeks coloring with lust.

Jamie had always seemed like someone who might have the nerve, the "why the fuck not" kind of daring that would let her go there with him, but he'd never imagined it would be *that fucking good*. He'd been so turned on by the whole thing he'd come after two and a half minutes, like a goddamn teenager.

And she'd been right there with him.

Dean felt himself harden, his dick too excited to be within easy distance of its number one fantasy. He couldn't believe they were actually doing this, and he wanted to ravage her as much as he wanted to savor her. To worship every inch, the way he'd dreamed about for so long.

She'd wanted it for six years too.

It shocked him, when she said that. He'd tried to find the words, some way to acknowledge he'd felt the same way. But it had been a risky moment, one that reminded him how much was at stake here, and Jamie had been smart to push past it.

They weren't here to have feelings. They were here to fuck, plain and simple.

Well, he could give her that. He could fuck her until she couldn't see straight. And as for him, he could let himself exist in this bubble of sunlight and cotton and her soft breathing a bit longer. They were out of town. Road trip rules applied. He could enjoy being like this with her for a little while.

Dean walked his fingers down the ladder of her ribs and teased over the hollow by her hip. Part of him wanted to see if he could get her hot enough to put on a show for him. He'd missed watching her touch herself last night because he was too busy trying to hold off. Looking at that wouldn't have given him a shot in hell of lasting.

Later. Right now, he wanted to rock her world again.

Her breathing pattern shifted when his thumb found her cleft. Slowly coming out of sleep, she rolled onto her back. He parted her soft flesh with a teasing caress, opening her up for him.

She whispered his name. It wasn't a word. It was a plea.

He stroked with firm, even circles, reveling in the unabashed noises of pleasure he drew from her, in the music of Jamie unraveled. It was like a drug, knowing he could get her there, and he drank in her startled gasps until her nails were digging into his arms and she was falling apart beneath him.

"Dean. Jesus Christ."

An aftershock went through her. She brought a hand up to cover her face, but he pulled it away. A pink flush covered her cheeks. Her smile was mixed with a sudden shyness, curls a mess, eyes downcast. It was that deviant angel look again—half innocence, half pure sin, the perfect mix of sexpot and girl next door.

"You okay?" he asked.

"No. I'm dead. You've killed me."

"Death by orgasm. I could think of worse."

She giggled and pressed her face into his chest. Dean chuckled, a stupid wide grin on his face. It was weird, smiling this much. Like his mouth had forgotten how. He curled a lock of her hair around his fingers and pulled the strand until it became a taut line, then watched it spring into a spiral again.

"I love that your hair does that."

Jamie groaned. "I hate my hair. It's ridiculous."

"It's adorable." He tugged lightly until she looked up at him. "And so are you."

It was probably more than he should've said, but it was true.

She grinned and stretched. He tracked his gaze down her

body. He'd gone down to half-mast, but it wouldn't take much to fix that.

"What time is it?" She looked toward the clock on the nightstand and bolted upright. "Eight o'clock? I slept until eight o'clock?"

Dean propped his head up on his arm. "I wasn't aware we were on a schedule."

"We're not. It's just..." She turned back to him, wide-eyed. "I haven't slept this late in a long time."

He couldn't help but smirk. "I think you were tired."

"Guess so." She ran a palm over his stomach, one finger dipping lower in a figure-eight tease. "Do I get to play again this morning?"

Fuck, yes.

"Depends." He relaxed back onto the pillows, folding his arms behind his head. "You willing to play in the shower?"

She followed his moves, feint for parry, leaning over him. "I spend half my life underwater. You think I don't know how to have fun when I'm wet?"

Oh, that was so happening. "Get your ass in the bathroom, Matthews."

One long shower later, both of them satisfied and starving beyond belief, they were having a late breakfast in the hotel restaurant.

"We should probably eat something with protein," Jamie said. "You know, to recover our strength."

Dean laughed and checked over the menu. The prices were higher than he'd expected.

"Omelets are the cheapest," she added, not meeting his eyes. "And the most likely to keep us full for a while."

It pierced through him, this knowledge that she was cutting costs for him, something she probably never had to do on her own. She'd said it so casually too, like it was too insubstantial to warrant eye contact.

He appreciated the relief her suggestion brought.

And he absolutely fucking hated it.

It had been a sobering week for the business, as a depressingly detailed review of the books had shown. But Dean knew it was pointless to make any suggestions to his father, and he'd been happy to get away for a few days and not deal with the pressure. He'd coughed up the cost of the room, taking a chunk out of his paycheck to cover it, figuring he could continue to survive on PB and J and cereal until the next one came in. He'd nearly asked Jamie to look for a less expensive place, but offering her a glimpse into his financial state would've been too serious a blow to his pride.

He didn't want her to know how bad things were.

His mood changed when they finished eating and went outside. The inn was pressed up against the bay, the surface of the water like crystal, the landscape behind them alive with the robust colors of autumn.

"Why don't you take some pictures today?" Jamie asked when they climbed into his truck. "I saw your camera in the back, and it seems like a nice day for it."

Dean didn't answer at first, busying himself by starting the engine and letting it idle, not wanting to run it too hard in the cold. He hadn't planned on using the camera again. He'd wiped the memory card after having the pharmacy save the images of Sean's wedding to a flash drive, then charged up the battery with the intention of selling the stupid thing altogether.

It was a part of his life he needed to bury, shove dirt over its grave and walk away from for good. But Jamie's request made him want to keep that casket open a little while longer.

"You could get a shot of me sprawled out on some old car," she joked.

Dean huffed out a laugh, his sex drive exhausted enough to file the idea away for later. A different kind of thrill ratcheted up his pulse, one that involved revving engines, classic tunes, and the chance to capture it all on film.

What harm could it do? If road trip rules applied to him and Jamie, they could apply to taking pictures too. He could go back to his regularly scheduled programming when they got home.

"Okay," he said as he pulled out of the lot. "You talked me into it."

It seemed like all of New Hampshire had come out for the fair. Dean found parking on a side street and retrieved his camera. They paid their entrance fees and treaded toward the lines of shiny bumpers. Rows of classic cars gleamed in the sun, their hoods lifted, colorful paint jobs shining.

Jamie plowed through the carpet of leaves covering the ground, kicking them in the air as she walked.

"We here to look at anything specific?" she asked.

"Nah. I just wanted to see all these things of beauty before their owners put them into storage for the season."

"Things of beauty?"

"Hell yeah." Dean leaned into the interior of a Model T, snapping a shot of its shiny white-and-red steering wheel. "You don't see it?"

"Not really. It just looks old."

"They are old, but someone took the time to polish them up and help them reclaim their former glory." He nabbed a shot of a toddler being hefted up by a parent, a look of wonder in her eyes as she peeked inside a vehicle built decades before she was born.

"Is that what you want to do?" she asked. "Fix up old cars?"

Dean hesitated. He devoted so much energy to ignoring what he wanted. Talking about what he did want was like ripping a bandage off a painful, oozing scar.

"Maybe." He kept his tone light, not letting his words touch that nerve. "I mean, it's the art to them that I like. Not fixing up busted wrecks for the lowest price."

"You did always like art."

Dean lifted his camera again, and kept his gaze trained through the viewfinder. It was so much easier to be honest with a lens between him and the outside world.

"Yeah. I did."

"Why'd you stop?"

The question was a punch he didn't have time to see coming, one he needed a minute to recover from. Several heartbeats passed before he could reply.

"I had to."

"Why?"

"I need you in the garage, son. I just wanted to make sure you realized that."

Dean swallowed. "Because of my dad."

They stopped walking. He lowered the camera when Jamie stepped in close. Despite the people and conversations and music around them, everything seemed to get quiet.

"What did he do?" she asked.

He tried to keep in the anger, the frustration at having been chained to something he didn't hate but could no longer love, not when he'd never had the option of choosing it.

"He told me photography was a great hobby and all, but that was it. The garage was my future."

She frowned. "You didn't ever tell him no?"

Dean shook his head and looked out at the cars, the people. Everything except Jamie's concerned expression.

"It's a family business. I couldn't walk away from that, especially after what my father put into it. He lost his marriage over it, all to keep it alive for me. I owed it to him to give it my all. So that's what I did."

Even though it felt more like a prison sentence than anything else.

He didn't tell her the rest. About exactly when that decree had been handed down. How it had made him end things with her when it was the opposite of what he wanted.

Jamie fit her hand snugly around his and squeezed. His gaze dropped to hers.

"Come on," she said with a smile. "Show me more of what you love about these old wrecks so we can go have some real fun."

Her words made his cock twitch. It felt good, to let her pull him into being playful again.

"You didn't have enough fun this morning?"

"Not *that* kind of fun." She pointed toward the fairgrounds. "There's a carousel over there. We're not going back to the hotel until we've eaten a ton of cotton candy and then nearly puked it up on one of the rides."

He tugged her close so his lips hovered by her ear. "No offense to cotton candy or anything, but fucking you until you're screaming sounds like a lot more fun to me."

She pushed him away and started walking, but she was blushing, her ears bright pink. Man, he liked knowing he got to her. Dean chuckled and followed her into the crowd.

They trekked through the cars and he took tons of photographs, gawking over collector car profiles and winning stickers in the windshields. They came upon a '54 Packard Clipper convertible, the owner beside it with a white beard and a radio playing Warrant's "Cherry Pie". He'd heard the song more times in the garage than he could count.

Jamie recognized it right away and began singing along. Dean raised an eyebrow.

"What? Sean was always blasting big hair band music," she said, then asked the owner if Dean could take a picture of her in the car.

He obliged, and she hopped into the backseat, sprawling herself across the leather in a way that made Dean wonder why the hell he'd let her leave the hotel room in the first place.

Once they'd made their way through the rest of the vehicles, she dragged him to the midway, gleeful as she clung to the solid mane of a ceramic horse. She asked him to join her, but he elected to stay back and take pictures.

Only half of them were of her.

She bought them a funnel of spun sugar after that to share. It was the size of her head, and she happily ate more than her half, licking the sticky remains off her fingers when she finished. She tugged him to a shooting game next and won herself a teddy bear. Triumphant, Jamie blew air off the tip of her plastic gun and winked at him, saying the cowgirl boots she had on helped her do it.

Dean laughed and took in what she was wearing when she turned around to claim her toy. Light brown boots, leggings that clung to every luscious curve, a thick purple sweater that outlined her hourglass shape.

Somewhere in the back of his mind, Dean realized how nicely she always dressed, but the larger portion of his brain was fixated on how she'd ushered him into the bathroom when she'd gotten dressed that morning, not letting him see what she was wearing underneath it yet.

He was like a ticking time bomb, wanting to get her back to the room and find out.

They made it back to the front end of the fairgrounds, and Jamie spun out in the middle of it, her grin encompassing a world of childlike awe. Dean stepped back to watch her twirl, everything behind her a rainbow of lights and toys and balloons. She tossed him her teddy bear and ran to jump in a leaf pile, then gathered two armfuls of crunchy leaves and sent them flying.

He tucked the stuffed animal under his arm and lifted his

camera to catch the moment—Jamie with her face upturned toward the sky, her skin clear and bright, curls wild and hands high above her head as a shower of oranges, reds and browns rained softly down to the ground around her.

She looked like freedom.

That was always her, always what she was to him, while he'd had shackles locked around his wrists since he learned how to shave.

She did it again, and that same hollow yearning he'd been clobbered by at the wedding slammed into his chest. He finally recognized the emotion for what it was, and summed it up into one single word:

Mine.

He wanted her to be his. It was a fierce kind of possession he'd never felt for anyone.

He wanted more than Jamie shivering underneath him, though. He wanted to take the way she made him feel, bottle it and bring it home with him, and never let her go. But Jamie didn't belong in his world, one filled with long hours and always hunting for the lowest costs. She belonged here, in lazy mornings spent at lakeshore inns, in Saturday afternoons full of color. This weekend was a dream, a step outside reality, a brief glimpse into a future that would never exist for them.

He could never give her the kind of life she deserved.

"I haven't done this in forever," she said, running to jump in another pile. "I always hated fall, but here it doesn't seem so bad."

Good. It was better that she didn't notice him watching her. Much better.

He took a longer route driving them back, enjoying the way the road spooled out before them. Traffic slowed at the mouth of the lake, and she asked him to stop when they neared an Italian joint across from the water.

"Let's get pizza," she said. "I've already destroyed my diet for the weekend with the cotton candy. Why not ruin it entirely?"

"I thought you were on my case about taking off a few pounds," he said, pulling into a spot on the side of the road.

Her hand was already on the door handle. "I'll work it off you later."

The sun had begun inching its way down to the tree line by the time their pie was ready. Dean offered to kick down the flatbed so they could watch the sunset. There was enough room back there, if they sat on the edge. She'd happily agreed, and they ate with their legs dangling over the open gate, looking out at the water.

"You really should keep taking pictures," Jamie said.

Dean's stomach tightened. He thought they'd left that conversation behind them. "I don't have time for it anymore."

She was quiet for a moment, thoughtful as she munched on her crust, then asked, "What if you could combine photography and the business?"

"What do you mean?"

"Well, people with cars like the ones we saw today need parts, right?"

"Usually, yeah."

"And you know how to find them. If you got the parts and fixed up the cars, you could photograph them after. Maybe make it a part of the business."

"It's not that simple." He didn't mean to be shutting her down. It was just something he'd thought of before. "Offering custom refurbishment requires cash. And labor. And a place to do it all." There was enough work to do on the building they were in without having to find another one.

"Couldn't you start with a few small jobs?" she asked. "There've got to be more clients like the one you were shopping for yesterday. Ones who've bought classic cars that need fixing. Couldn't you advertise being available for work like that?"

Dean mulled it over. She had a point. And there were people out there who wanted to buy a classic, but didn't know how to fix it up. He could hunt down the parts, offer the guys at the shop extra hours to help work on them, and take photos of the finished projects when they were done. Connor could easily add a gallery to the website, and put some of his supernatural tech mojo into it so it reached the search engines.

"Maybe," he said. "There's still the problem of space, though."

She reached up and flicked his forehead. "You live in a warehouse, dumbass. Couldn't you use some of that space?"

Dean flicked her back on the shoulder, then rubbed the still-stinging spot between his eyes. He *could* use the first floor, if he managed to clean out enough of his father's crap. Maybe it would be something the old man would go for, if Dean could come up with a plan that cost the least amount of overhead.

Suddenly, the evening felt like an echo of that one back in high school, bright and brimming over with possibilities.

"Dumbass, huh?" He grinned. "Since when did you turn into a life coach?"

"It's a lot easier to come up with answers for other people's problems than it is for my own."

The sarcasm lacing her tone felt heavy. Dean took another bite of pizza and bumped her shoulder with his.

"You gonna talk about it, or what?"

He'd had enough with tiptoeing around the shit that was obviously going down between her and her family. He'd pulled back the dusty cobwebs of his past for her. It was time she threw in her chips too.

She tossed a half-eaten piece of pizza back in the box and

wiped off her hands. "I've been offered a promotion. Assistant Aquatics Director at the community center."

"Assistant director? That's a big step up."

She snorted. "Oh, yeah. It's my life's dream."

Dean studied her face. She was looking down, fussing with the tassels on her scarf.

"Art was your dream, right?" he asked.

Jamie swallowed. Stared at the water. "Fashion. I wanted to be a fashion designer."

"Why didn't you go after it?"

She shrugged, indifferent, her expression muted. "I tried. It didn't work out."

Dean suppressed the urge to tug on her hair, to use it to make her talk. He wouldn't, not after last night. One look at her lust-crazed eyes and there'd be little he could think of other than getting inside her as quickly as possible.

"No clamming up on me, honey," he said. "I revealed my big secret. Now it's your turn."

Jamie rolled her eyes, but the humor felt forced. "It's no secret. I applied to some art schools and got rejected."

She leaned back, balancing her weight on her elbows. Dean refused to look at the long, lean line of her body, and focused on her face instead, on the brightness that had suddenly shorted out. It was exactly like when she'd dodged his question years ago, when she told him about the scholarship she wasn't sure she wanted.

"If it wasn't a secret, why didn't you tell me about it back then?"

A tight frown pinched the edges of her mouth. "It was too hard to talk about. Not when my brothers had all gotten into Ivy League schools."

"I never thought you cared about stuff like that."

"Yeah, I know. Crazy, fun Jamie, right? Why would she care

about looking as smart as her brothers?" She offered him a smile, but its brilliance was dampened by her eyes, missing their usual luster.

Jamie looked away but the fissure was still there, the pain she'd covered up with humor and smiles suddenly all too obvious. It made sense now—her bratty, prankster side was nothing more than a defense mechanism. A way to get attention when she'd been eclipsed by her brothers' accomplishments.

Funny. They were polar opposites, but exactly the same—her family's success was hanging over her, while he'd been enshrouded by the failure of his.

"You couldn't get a job somewhere in fashion?" he asked. Christ, she had a college degree. That had to get her somewhere.

"Nah. I'd have to go back to school and major in it. And move to New York if I wanted to get anywhere." She rubbed her fingers together. "*Ker-ching, ker-ching.*"

"Oh, come on. You're telling me your parents wouldn't support you?"

Her eyes went even darker. "I've lived off their good graces for a while now. I think my welcome is running out."

She sat up and rubbed her hands over her arms. Dean wasn't sure if it was because she was cold or needed comforting.

He wasn't sure if it was his place to offer her solace for either.

"It's okay," she said. "The job at the center is good money. It'll pay me enough so I can finally cover my own bills and move out. And swimming does make me happy."

"No, it doesn't."

Her gaze snapped to his. She started to argue, but Dean shook his head.

"That's not the face of someone who's happy."

"Okay. Maybe I'm not *ecstatic*, but I'm content. It's like your hierarchy says. Be okay with the status quo, and life will be good, right?"

For a minute, Dean hated the theory he'd relied on, not liking it at all when it came to Jamie. When it clenched its jaws around the image he'd always had of her—happy and carefree, never held down by anything.

It was like gravity reversed, to hear she'd become as trapped as he was.

"It would've been nice, though," she added softly. "To work in fashion. It's transformative, the way one outfit can turn you into something else. Let you *be* someone else."

Dean's pulse stalled. He stared at her. "You wish you were someone else?"

Jamie gave him a weak smile. "I wanted to do something meaningful. To have a life that was more than smelling like chlorine and constantly having swimmers' ear." She laughed quietly and shrugged. "I wasn't good enough for it."

Something inside Dean snapped. He gathered the remains of their dinner into the box and chucked it into a bin on the street, anger pooling like battery acid. She thought it was okay that she'd given up her dream, but it wasn't *okay*. Not in the slightest. It wasn't okay that she was disappointed in her life.

That she thought she wasn't good enough.

He wrapped one hand around the back of her neck and drew her gaze up, not caring if it was appropriate. If it broke the boundaries of their weekend rules. She needed to hear this.

"You listen to me," he said. "Don't you ever say you're not good enough for something. That you don't deserve to have a life that's amazing and exciting. Don't even think it. Because if there's anyone who deserves the most incredible future possible, it's you."

Jamie blinked. Her mouth dropped open slightly, brows lifting with surprise and something else he didn't have the brainpower to put his finger on.

Dean kept going, honesty bubbling up inside him, a hole poked through a dam.

"When I look at you, I see that girl I knew as a kid. Someone who was always smiling, always happy, and has stayed like that, no matter what. You're like this one single bright fucking spot of sunshine I have in a life that pretty much sucks otherwise, so don't you dare wish you were anyone else, or think you can't have what you want. You should have *everything* you want, Jamie. Everything."

Her eyes brightened and glossed over, brown turned to gold in the waning sunlight.

Then she smiled, leaned in close and whispered, "Take me back to the hotel, Dean."

TEN

Dean twisted away, boots hitting the concrete before Jamie said another word. He had the gate folded up by the time she'd hopped into the front, and swung himself into the driver's seat, jamming the key in the ignition. He grabbed her hand when he started to drive, pulled it onto his lap and held it firmly against his thigh. He needed to touch her, something to cut the tension until he got her back to the room.

It apparently wasn't enough for her. She inched her fingertips down and swept them over his fly.

Dean groaned and clenched his jaw, his eyes on the road. "Don't do that."

Jamie laughed softly. She sidled next to him and kissed behind his ear, down his neck, teeth a rough chafe against the sensitive spot at his shoulder she knew so well.

"Fuck." He shuddered, hips shifting forward. "You're gonna get us killed, doing that."

She licked over the spot she'd bitten. "Then drive faster."

He grunted, hand gripping hers more tightly. He took the camera with him when they reached the hotel lot, too impatient to waste time locking it up in the back. They hurried through the lobby, Dean's fingers wound tightly around hers. Finally at their room, he dragged the key card from his back pocket and opened the door with one hand. Jamie barely had time to catch her breath before he dropped the camera bag to the floor, shut the door and slammed her up against it.

"Too many clothes," he snarled. "You're wearing too many fucking clothes."

"I like my clothes."

Snarky words, but she was panting despite them. Dean skimmed the bottom of her sweater up her sides, pushing the fabric over her head.

"I like them too. But I'll like them better off you." He yanked off his shirt, tossed it to the ground and growled, "Shoes."

Jamie complied, eagerly kicking them off. Dean's brain buzzed as he stepped out of his boots, everything she'd told him about her severed dreams settling into a low hum like a rattling engine in his thoughts. He hoped she'd be able to find a way out of the life she'd let herself get tangled in. That someday she'd get everything she aspired for, and have that exciting life down in New York City.

But not right now.

Right now, she was his.

He gripped her leggings and dragged them down, some kind of caveman, testosterone-filled urge taking over him, wanting to prove she wouldn't be able to "get him out of her system". That two nights with him would only make her want him more.

He knew he shouldn't want that, because he refused to trap her any more than she'd already trapped herself, but *God*, he couldn't help it.

Dean moved to stand, stopping short when he saw the scrap of fabric at the apex of her thighs: a triangle of sheer white, laced up like a corset and held together with a tiny bow.

"Jesus," he breathed.

So this was what she'd been hiding from him. Thank fuck he hadn't known about it, or he would've been hard all day. His brain registered that her bra matched too, but he couldn't draw his eyes away from the mouth-watering sight in front of him.

Curling his hands around her hips, he brought his mouth to her cloth-covered slit. Her skin was smooth and soft beneath it, bare except for a tiny strip of hair.

He kissed her fully, over and over, and she dropped her hands to clutch his hair. Dean closed his eyes and concentrated on the way she moved, how she tried to gather more of the sensation, body arching off the wall. Every reaction notched his need to epic proportions, but he held it in check. Making her come wasn't enough. He wanted to take this glorious girl out of the corner she'd let herself get put in, and make her see herself the way he did.

He slid her panties down her legs, then stood and unclasped her bra. It landed in a pile with the rest of their clothes. He shucked his jeans and boxers, adding them to the mess, then finally kissed her.

Jamie clawed at his back, the pure hunger in her response jacking him up even higher. He palmed her thighs, hitching them up over his waist. She wrapped her legs around him, kissing him frantically as he walked them to the bed.

"How do you want it, Jamie?"

"I don't care," she said in between kisses. "Just take me."

He dug fingers into her backside, reveling in her hiss. "How? Specifically."

If tonight was going to be his last night with her, he was going to make it memorable.

She panted, cautious, then whispered, "From behind. Hard."

Fuck.

He eased her down to the floor. "Bend over the bed."

Jamie turned around, doing as she was told. Dean palmed his dick, unable to resist the urge to stroke at the sight of her ass on display. She looked over her shoulder, glanced at his slowly pumping fist and grinned.

He reached for a condom, quickly rolling it on. Another minute of that and this whole thing would be over before it even started.

Dean nudged her legs apart with his knee, then bent down to kiss the divots above her bottom and mapped her spine with his tongue.

Her hips flexed. "Please."

He ignored her plea and slipped his hands beneath her to cup her breasts, tweaking lightly at her nipples before sliding down lower. Teasing her flesh, he coaxed her open, thumbs light over her clit.

She whined and pushed back against him. Groaned his name.

He loved how turned on she was, how hungry and restless. That was how he wanted her—this time anyway.

Next time, he'd let her take what she needed.

With one hand on her hip to steady her, he eased inside her slick passage. Dean almost lost it within seconds, going stupid already with the feeling of hot and tight and so fucking good. He closed his eyes, trying to collect himself, because he was unraveling too quickly. If he looked at her, took in those fuckhot responses and let them hit home, he'd be a goner.

She whimpered, pressing back against him. The sound helped him find his control. He reopened his eyes and moved slowly, keeping his thrusts deep and even. Jamie cursed in pleasure as he surged and withdrew, surged and withdrew.

He halted before his next plunge, wanting to see what she would do, how frenzied he could make her. She hiked her chin over her shoulder, her gaze tiptoeing backward. When their eyes met, the connection was as sharp and hot if he'd sunk into her again.

"Fuck," she gasped. "I love it when you look at me like that."

He'd picked up on it before. The way one glance seemed to hold her still.

"You like being watched?" He thrust forward, an unhurried push that made her mouth drop open and her eyes slam shut. "My little exhibitionist?"

"I do, but...*oh*...not like that." She bit her lip, eyes opening again. Latching onto his. "I love the way you watch me. How you —*fuck*...how you see me."

What Jamie truly needed crystallized into focus. It wasn't just about being held down, about giving up control and letting go. It was that she'd spent a lifetime living in other people's shadows, and needed to be seen.

Dean slid a palm down her back and grabbed a fistful of her hair. She responded with another deep groan.

"I see you," he said. "I see what you want. What you crave."

He did. And he wanted to watch her absorb every last drop of it.

"Harder," she begged. "Please."

"You want it harder?"

"Yes."

Releasing her hair and hip, he leaned over her and whispered, "So do I."

A shuddered curse was all she had time for before he pushed her down onto the bed and dragged her arms behind her. He pinned her wrists together at the small of her back and secured them with one hand, then snatched her by the hair again, hard enough to lift her whole body. Jamie cried out and arched into the contorted shape he'd twisted her into, taking everything he gave her as he started a punishing rhythm.

It was ridiculously erotic, seeing her let loose like that. Dean's release bore down on him, his balls tightening, legs going stiff.

"Don't stop," she pleaded. "Don't...I'm going to...oh, God."

She didn't need to warn him. Her body told him for her, unable to hide it when her orgasm rocked through her. Her voice broke on a wail that lashed out at him, shattering his control and reducing him to an animal.

Lost to any thought other than the need to come, Dean urged her forward, one hand spanning her back as he pressed her firmly against the mattress. Climbing up on the bed behind her, he fucked into her hard and steady, hips pistoning with quick, ruthless moves. Her pussy surrounded him. So good, so deep. He had only seconds to enjoy the way her muffled moans matched his until pleasure shot up his spine. He snapped taut, his body taken hold by an orgasm so hot and intense it felt like whiplash.

Sated, he all but collapsed on top of her. His arms shook when he leaned down to kiss between her shoulder blades, tasting the salt of her sweaty skin.

Dean tossed the condom in the trash. Jamie turned over onto her back, head at the foot of the bed, arms draped over the edge of the mattress. She grinned wide, her arms stretched up above her head, back rolling like a cat. It reminded him of the way she'd sprawled out across the backseat of that car this afternoon.

"Don't move," he said.

Slipping his jeans and boxers back on, he retrieved his camera from where he'd left it by the door. Changing the settings to allow for the darkness of the room, he focused in on her. With her legs up in a lazy upside-down V, her knees swaying from side to side and her curls spilling everywhere, she was every bit the tainted angel of his teenage fantasies, the one who'd gone bad and liked it.

She lifted her chin and looked over at him. "What are you doing?"

Trying to capture how beautiful you are.

"What does it look like?" he asked. "Stay like that."

"These aren't going to end up on the Internet, are they?"

He scowled from behind the lens. As if he'd ever do that to her. "Of course not."

He hadn't thought far enough ahead to imagine what he'd do with the pictures after the weekend was over. He was simply compelled to record the moment. He'd think about the rest later.

She grew bashful when he got too close, giggling from behind lowered lashes.

"We could turn this into your own personal X-rated fashion show," she said.

"We could." He concentrated, needing to catch the demure look on her face.

"Yeah?"

"Sure. Go put something on for me."

Jamie scampered off the bed and knelt by her bag. Dean lounged back on the pillows while she dressed, keeping his eyes off her so he got the full effect when she was done.

"How's this?"

He glanced up. She'd topped a black bra and panties with a sexy gray-and-black pinstripe jacket. She'd put on a necklace too —a long line of dark beads that spilled over her cleavage and kissed her belly button.

And he was ready for round two. Dean swallowed.

"Where'd you think you'd be wearing that?"

She flashed him a snide grin. "It comes with pants, smartass," she said. "I didn't know what was out here. Lifeguards always come prepared."

"Isn't that the Boy Scouts?"

"Whatever." Jamie crawled onto the bed and smiled, a sex kitten on her knees. "You like?"

Like didn't cover it.

He scooted down until he was lying flat on the bed. "Put your hands behind your head."

She followed his instructions, bunching her hands in her hair so several soft strands fell around her face. The move lifted her breasts, beads dangling between them. She puckered her lips like a supermodel, but was unable to hold the expression for long before dissolving into laughter.

It was going to make an incredible shot.

"Lose the jacket."

She drew it off slowly, one sleeve at a time. He kept hitting the shutter button until she'd tossed it to the floor. His dick couldn't handle the striptease, hard again already and fighting the constraints of his jeans. Dean pushed a palm down to stifle the ache, but it only made everything worse, something he could tell Jamie caught by the way she raised her eyebrows, the corner of her mouth turned upward.

"I want to take a few pictures too," she said. "Can I?"

He looked at her for a minute, at the gleam in her eyes.

One night. One night to be whatever she wanted. To give her whatever he could.

He wordlessly handed the camera over.

She bounced back onto her bottom, delighted. "Okay, Trescott. Strip."

Feeling his own cheeks color, Dean rose up on his knees. He couldn't look at the camera, surprised by his own embarrassment, especially when he unzipped his fly and his cock made an appearance beneath the cotton.

Jamie made a soft noise of appreciation. Dean looked up to see that she'd trapped her lower lip between her teeth. Her gaze raked over him like heat.

"I think the working out has done you good," she said with a coy smile. "But then again, I liked the way you were before too. You're kinda like a giant teddy bear."

Dean froze. "I am *not* like a teddy bear."

"Yes, you are. A big, bad sexy one. With tattoos instead of fur."

He laughed. Jamie smiled from behind the camera and twirled a finger in the air, as if to say *get on with it.*

Enjoying the ego stroke of her attention, he hooked his thumbs into the backs of his jeans and boxers, and pushed everything down, one inch at a time. She took a couple more quick shots, then stopped when he rid himself of his clothes entirely.

The camera forgotten, she put it on the edge of the bed and crawled over to him, but it wasn't his throbbing dick that she reached for. Her fingers light, she began tracing the ink on his arm.

"Is this okay?" she asked.

He nodded and stayed silent, letting her touch, watching as she took him in. She caressed the sleeve, soft touches to the thorny spines he'd had drawn into his flesh.

"Barbed wire. I guess that's kind of a warning, huh?" she asked. "A metaphorical 'do not enter'."

He chuckled. It was cliché, but true.

Light fingers stroked over his ribs. "Birds flying away. Freedom? Or wishing for it."

Dean took a breath. She was right on the money.

"Both," he said, but the word came out strained.

She moved to his other shoulder, following the map in his skin, but she wasn't asking about them the way other women had, wanting his practiced stories. She wasn't using it as a treasure hunt either, a ploy to get to something better.

She was reading him, as clearly as if he'd labeled his ink with signs.

"A compass rose, but there's no cardinal points, no north or south. You're drifting. Lost."

His throat went tight. No woman had ever questioned why his compass had no direction, why he'd gotten a tattoo of something that was supposed to guide him without including the symbols that let it.

It reminded him to stay the course. Not follow his heart.

And Jamie had figured it out without even asking.

As much as he tried to shut it out, Dean knew this was what he'd been missing. The intimacy, the feeling of being *known*—that was what had been absent from every sweaty encounter he'd had. He also knew the reason that night with Jamie back in high school had been so special.

It was because she'd looked at him like this, her eyes open and full of wonderment.

Everything snapped into perfect focus when her hand came to rest over the stars on his heart. He could screw every woman in the world blind and he'd never shake her from his system.

It was always going to be her.

He took both her hands in his before she had a chance to ask what the design meant and placed them on his chest.

"Take what you want, Jamie."

He hoped she'd realize he was repeating her words from the day before, that he was saying it because he wanted to give her everything. Because he wanted her to feel in control for once, to know she could have what she wanted, and that he was hers for the taking until morning.

Jamie took a condom from the nightstand, placed it beside them on the bed and climbed on top of him. The warm satin covering her skin was a sinful slide against his cock. When she leaned down to kiss him, her necklace dragged over his chest. Dean wasn't sure if it was the scrape of the beads or her mouth that made him shudder. She rose up to shimmy out of her panties, and then she was fitting the condom over him.

She pressed down, lowering her body until he was fully seated. His eyes nearly rolled back in his head.

"Ah, *fuck*, Jamie."

Dean fisted his hands by his sides to stop himself from taking over. Instead he cataloged her every shiver, every moan as she rose up and dropped down, tucking her reactions away for safe keeping.

Her soft breaths grew faster as she worked herself above him and said, "Touch me, Dean."

He offered her his hands. "Show me where."

She took his hands in hers and drew them to her hips. He stroked her skin, squeezing when she asked him to with a gentle press of her fingers. She tugged one hand a little harder, pulling it to where they were joined.

"Wait," he whispered, tugging her fingers in return. "Let me watch you first."

He had to. He fucking had to see that, just once.

She chewed her lip, and he helped the decision along by circling his hips beneath her, changing the angle so her next downward movement rubbed his tip along that crazy-sensitive place inside her. Jamie grunted, nearly doubling over, and then she was touching herself, tiny up-and-down motions that quickly got her where she needed to go.

It got him there too. The image was too fucking hot for his brain or his body to handle.

"Dean." She clutched his fingers. "You. Please."

He knew what she needed, and he wanted to give it to her. Sitting up, he took over for her, his hand between them and stroking until she trembled. She was the one to grab his hair when she came, holding on as her lips bruised his with rough, violent kisses. Dean worked her clit until her grip loosened, then clamped his eyes shut as he followed her over the edge. He couldn't keep them open and witness what he knew would be the last time he ever saw her like this, beautiful and satisfied and panting to quiet above him.

He didn't open his eyes again until she'd stretched out on the bed. Dean threw the condom in the trash and shut off the light. Curling up beside her in the darkness, he reminded himself of the final rule of a road trip:

Eventually, the trip had to end.

ELEVEN

J amie didn't want the weekend to be over.

Snuggled under the covers with Dean on Sunday morning, her back against his chest and some old cartoon he'd been completely stoked to find playing on the TV, she felt relaxed. Content.

Maybe it was being away from home, trading ocean and sand for the sheltering peaks of the mountains and the flat calm of the lake. Or maybe it was being at the fair yesterday, kicking up leaves, enjoying fall for once. Whatever it was, an understanding had taken root, saturating her thoughts as the day went on. She realized that Portland wasn't holding her back, and neither was her brothers' success.

The problem was all her.

She'd boxed herself into the life she was living, giving up on anything else because she'd tried once and failed, but Dean made her feel confident, something she'd never felt any place other than a pool. What he said in his truck yesterday about her deserving an amazing life showed her how silly it was to have given up when she'd hit one bump in the road. And when the sunlight came in through the curtains this morning, warming their tangled bodies on the bed, Jamie finally figured out what she wanted.

She wanted to go back to school for a degree in fashion. To spend her time learning about materials and textiles, to get over her fear of working with a sewing machine and see what kinds of designs she could create. To tell her parents about the program she'd looked into, and ask them to support her, the way they'd supported her brothers. She wanted to grab hold of her dreams and chase after them, but school wasn't the only thing that would give her the exciting life she'd always wanted.

She wanted Dean too.

They'd agreed on one time, but being with him like this had changed the game. It wasn't only the way they were able to laugh and talk, or how incredible the sex was, how she'd finally been able to feel wild and let go. It was the feeling of being *seen*, something she'd never had with anyone else, something she couldn't have had without the years of history the two of them shared. And last night, that final time, holding on to each other as the pleasure built until they splintered apart—it felt like so much more than a quick romp in the sheets. More than some dirty little secret they'd stolen away to share and would never talk about again.

It felt like everything.

She stroked Dean's knee over the sheet covering them. What he'd said about his dad answered so many questions. He didn't think he was supposed to make his mark on the world, or come up with anything creative and beautiful. With the weight of business on his shoulders, he thought he had to fall in line and do his duty to his family, but Jamie could see the boy he once was on the inside. The one who'd handed her a handful of hopes over a rusty art table and asked her what she thought.

He could do so much more. Could *be* so much more. And she could show him that.

He could ground her and she could lift him up. They were perfect for each other. How had she never realized that?

She'd thought they were too much alike to ever balance out: both of them relationship-hoppers, unable to commit. But they'd both lost sight of what they wanted, both of them lost. And it wasn't only sex drawing her back to him like a lighthouse on the shore. Six years of being unable to connect to other guys was all because she wanted *him*. Because despite everything they'd been through, she still wanted to be around him. Still liked him.

Loved him?

A tingle raced from her shoulders to her toes. It made sense, now, why she'd never tried to start a life somewhere else. It wasn't because she'd gotten stuck. It was because something inside her had known this was possible.

That she and Dean could be amazing together, if they let themselves.

The cartoon ended, and he shut off the TV. He didn't say anything, just ran his fingertips down her arms and marked her neck with a soft, wet kiss. Lifting a hand to her breast, he circled gently, easing his palm over her nipple until it rose up under his touch.

Jamie shivered, her reaction instantaneous. Involuntary. Her body had known for years that it wanted him. It had just taken time for her brain to catch up.

He pulled the covers back with his other hand, all that muscle and ink crisscrossing over her belly as he palmed her thigh and spread her open.

"Let me?" she asked, reaching around to thread her arm between them.

He shook his head, kissing beneath her ear as his fingers inched lower. "Just you."

Her ability to protest vanished when he teased her. Circled. Delved between her lips and slid inside. Jamie was amazed she could take any more considering how many times he'd made her come, but she was ready for it, her pussy wet and aching after one deep pump.

He returned to her clit and worked her quickly, alternating wide circles that skidded by her most sensitive spots with rubbing directly against them. Her body arched with little ripples of pleasure, his warm breath at her neck making her melt. He brought her to the edge and kept her there, and Jamie clung to him, her heels pedaling against the mattress until he sped up and pressed down and *ohhh, fuck.*

Her voice cracked when she came, his name the only thing she could say, his arms the only thing she could cling to as he broke her apart and put her back together again.

She could barely breathe, let alone speak when she returned to earth. Her heart was thumping so fast because of what she was about to say, but he'd told her she was the only bright spot in his life, that she should have everything she wanted, so Jamie imagined she was standing at the edge of a diving board, and jumped.

"Can I tell you something?"

"Hmmm?" His mouth was still pressed against her ear, one hand on her belly, the other playing with her hair.

"There's another reason why I never pushed myself to go to New York."

"What's that?"

"Because it would've meant I'd be too far away from you."

A short exhale was her only answer. Silent, he twirled a tiny bit of her hair around a finger and pulled it straight. When it sprang back into place, Dean squeezed her once tightly, then shifted behind her. Jamie sat forward, letting him move, expecting a conversation to follow.

He stood up and started to dress instead, keeping his back to her.

"Dean," she began softly.

"Yeah?"

Did we screw everything up?

Am I still your favorite girl?

Did that ever really mean anything?

"Did I...are you...mad?"

"Course not." His boxers and jeans were already on. "Why would I be mad?"

"Cause you're acting..." She watched him drag a gray T-shirt over his head. "Weird."

He turned around. A casual mask was fixed on his face.

"It's cool. We've just gotta get moving. Check-out time." He threw her a smile and waved toward the bathroom. "I'm gonna wash up."

The smile didn't reach his eyes.

They barely spoke the entire drive back. When he pulled to a stop in front of her house and cut the engine, Jamie stared at the driveway. A chasm had opened between them, and she didn't know how to close it.

She turned to face him. He didn't move, just stared out the windshield, his jaw tense.

"I meant what I said in the hotel," she said quietly.

Dean's fist made contact with the steering wheel, three short, staccato strikes before he sighed heavily and ran the heel of his palm over his head.

"I thought we were coming back here like it never happened," he said. "That we were getting it out of our systems and leaving it behind us."

The air in the cramped space of the cab grew thin. There had to have been something wrong with the ventilation, because Jamie suddenly couldn't breathe.

"Is that still what you want?" she asked.

"It's what we agreed to, isn't it? One time, and then we'd go back to normal."

Right. She was supposed to act normal around him. Not like her heart was trying to claw its way out of her chest. She'd forgotten he was still the legendary Dean Trescott. There could be half a dozen women back here waiting for him. Oats waiting to be sowed.

"I thought maybe, something might have changed."

It felt foolish to have thought that, now. To think anything would be different for him. The whole weekend was her suggestion after all. She'd planned to take back control. Get what she wanted. Scratch the itch and move on.

She hadn't expected to realize she was in love with him.

Dean looked at her with eyes that had gone flat and dark, the coal-gray color of the ocean before a storm. "I don't know what you want me to say, Jamie."

Of course he didn't. Because he didn't feel the same way. His rejection felt like Parsons and F.I.T. all over again.

Dear Ms. Matthews, We regret to inform you that Dean Trescott doesn't want you, either.

The tears threatened. She reached for the door handle.

"Nothing. You don't have to say anything." She shoved the door open, slammed it shut and waited on the pavement.

Dean dug his hand through his hair and banged a fist against the roof. When he came out to pull open the truck box, she yanked her bag from it and started up her walkway.

"Jamie," he called out.

It hurt to turn around. He seemed so far away on the other side of his truck, hands jammed into his pockets, his hair lifting on a breeze. Leaves skittered across the pavement around him like tiny red tumbleweeds.

"We still good?"

Her heart stopped beating.

She couldn't believe he was asking her that. She couldn't believe she was stupid enough to think he'd say anything different.

She never wanted to hear those words again.

"Of course, Dean," she said, not caring if he heard the sarcasm in her voice. "We're always good."

Jamie stormed toward her house, too angry to feel sadness or regret. Too angry to do anything except walk away from him and never, ever look back.

* * *

Five days later, Jamie came home from her Friday shift at the center ravenous and completely exhausted. It was only midafternoon but her stomach was rumbling like she hadn't eaten in days. She'd thrown herself into the workweek, picking up as many extra shifts as possible.

She'd needed the distraction.

Portland was a minefield, everything around her a tripwire, triggering memories of Dean. Halloween candy in the supermarket. Red-brown leaves on her lawn. That stupid bear she'd won at the fair, mocking her from her dresser.

She hadn't had the heart to get rid of it. It wasn't the bear's fault, after all. And it served as a reminder of how what she thought was real was only make-believe. The whole thing had been a false start, and she dove in headfirst without looking, when she should've known that hitting the bottom would be the end result all along.

It was behind her now. And she had a decision to make: take the job at the center, or turn it down.

Dean's easy dismissal of her feelings last weekend had shaken her confidence, making her second-guess everything she'd thought she could do. She couldn't trust the whim that had said *go back to school, make fashion your focus*, since the person who'd made her believe that was possible didn't actually want to be a part of her world.

Swimming had always been the easy fallback. But doing the easy thing wasn't sitting right with her anymore, either.

She had until Sunday to give her boss an answer.

Jamie made her way into the kitchen. Her mother was sitting at the table.

"Hey," she said. "We haven't seen much of you this week."

"Yeah, sorry. I've been working a lot." Jamie opened the fridge, searching for something that would take the least amount of effort to make.

"You hungry?"

No, she just liked sticking her face in forty-degree air after being underwater all day. "Starving."

"I have some leftovers from dinner with the board of trustees last night." She stood and shooed Jamie away from the fridge. "Sit. I'll heat it up for you."

Jamie couldn't remember the last time they'd sat here alone together. It was awkward, being like this now, but her mother was offering, and Jamie was too hungry and tired to come up with a reason to turn her down.

She sank into a chair and put her chin in her hands. "Where's Dad?"

"Still at the hospital." Her mother filled a plate with pasta from a Styrofoam container. "So, it seems you were back to your usual antics when the boys were home."

Jamie glanced up. The look being sent her way wasn't judgmental or disapproving. It seemed like a fact mission, a request for information.

"I only pulled a couple of pranks."

Her mother focused on the microwave. "I thought you were over that."

Jamie picked up a pen and started doodling on a napkin. She wanted to have been over it. She *should've* been. But the little kid inside had been waving stick figure drawings and stomping her foot.

Mommy, pay attention to me.

"I'm sorry," she said.

Her mother shrugged. "Don't apologize to me. I'm not the one whose wedding gifts you pretended were about to careen into the ocean."

Again, there was no sense of irritation in her tone. If anything, it sounded more like...humor? Jamie chanced another look in her mother's direction. Pursed lips had quirked up into a grin.

"It was a good joke, though," she said.

Laughter broke through the surface of Jamie's dour mood. It *was* a good joke, but she shouldn't have done that to Sean on his wedding day.

"I should tell him I'm sorry. It's just—"

The words got caught in her throat. Her muscles wound tight, that familiar tension seeping into her bones, the reminder that she hadn't lived up to any semblance of potential so powerful it was all she could do to keep herself in her chair.

"Having them home wasn't easy for me."

The microwave beeped. Jamie's mother brought the plate to the table and sat down across from her. "You want to tell me why?"

She put the pen down and picked up a fork, even though her appetite had suddenly taken a nosedive. She'd already put herself out there once this week. Having another soul-baring discussion wasn't exactly an enticing prospect.

But if she didn't say it now, she might never be able to.

"Because you're so proud of them. And you're not proud of me."

"You think I'm not proud of you?" she asked. "Why would you think that?"

The shock in her mother's voice took Jamie by surprise. As if her self-doubt was even crazier than anything else she'd said or done. But it was lip service. It had to be. Hearing her mother was proud of her was as strange as hearing she'd suddenly won Olympic Gold.

"I'm wild, silly Jamie, right?" She prepared herself for the quote. "The one who's 'never serious about anything'."

Her mother's lips scrunched to the side in a move Jamie often made herself. It was a nervous tendency she hadn't realized they shared.

"Yeah, I shouldn't have said that. I'm sorry."

The apology soothed some of Jamie's rattled nerves but she still felt raw, the mask of sarcasm and humor she so often wore peeled unceremoniously back and showing the mess she was inside.

"I'm a tough love kind of parent," her mother added. "The boys always had such thick skins, and you acted a lot like them. I didn't think you needed anything different."

Jamie looked down and swirled her dinner around on her plate, blinking back the hot sting of tears.

"I wanted you to *see* me."

Her voice broke. She tried to control her outburst, but the little-kid feeling was hard to combat. The one that said her brothers were always going to be better than her. That no matter what she'd done or how hard she'd tried, she'd ended up a failure.

Warm fingers brushed a lock of hair out of her eyes. "I see you. The swimmer. The fashion diva. The artist."

Her gaze snapped up. Her mother nodded at the napkin

Jamie had drawn a pantsuit on and smiled. She crossed her arms on the table and leaned in closer.

"I knew you didn't get into those art schools, you know. I saw the letters in the trash."

The plunge in Jamie's stomach was like jumping off the high board. She didn't remember throwing the letters out. She'd been so upset by her rejection that she'd been careless with the evidence.

"Why didn't you say something?" Jamie asked.

"I figured you'd talk about it when you were ready. Maybe I should've pushed more, but we did so much of that with your brothers. I didn't want to push you too."

Jamie could only blink. "Wait, what?"

Her mother laughed. "You think they all wanted to go to medical school? Sean was practically born with a stethoscope, but Brendan almost dropped out halfway through and Owen's not sure emergency medicine is what he wants to do anymore."

Her brothers, not perfect? Impossible.

"But Dad made them go?" she asked.

"He not-so-gently encouraged, maybe?"

"And he never did that with me."

The pervasive feeling that she wasn't good enough hovered again, a pin in a grenade.

"Not because we didn't think you could, if it was what you wanted. Because you've always been different, and we wanted you to make your own choices."

Another blink was all she could manage. What was happening here?

"So you really have been waiting for me to figure myself out."

"Yes, but not for you to become like the boys or your father. I wanted *you* to decide what you want."

Jamie studied the pasta growing cold on her plate. What the hell did she want?

She wasn't sure, but she was sick and tired of wallowing in the feeling that she'd never accomplish anything. And the idea of trying for a career in fashion still made her heartbeat quicken.

She wanted to trust that emotion, despite the way Dean's refusal had shaken her.

"I've been offered a promotion at the center," she said. "But I don't know if I want to take it."

"Okay," her mother said slowly. "If you don't want to swim then don't swim. But do *something*, Jamie. Because you're not staying at home forever."

It was a jibe, but a playful one. One said with a smile and her mother's weird brand of love. A tactless style of encouragement Jamie had inherited. Wasn't teasing the way she'd talked to Dean too?

The errant thought of happy times with him was another mine tripped over. The sudden moment of buoyancy deflated.

"Were people asking about me at the wedding?" she asked. "Why the last of the great Matthews clan was still living at home?"

Her mother snorted. "Please. Half the guests were too busy complaining about the band."

"Complaining?" Jamie asked. "The music rocked at the wedding. Sean has good taste."

A piqued eyebrow was followed by a teasing grin. "Did you just...*defend* your brother?"

Jamie sat back, astonished. "I guess I did."

Her mother plucked Jamie's fork from her fingers and stole a bite of pasta.

"The only thing people asked about you was whether or not anyone had broken your swim record yet," she said as she chewed. "And complimenting you when I told them who'd chosen the bridesmaid dresses."

A smile tugged at the edges of her lips. Jamie stared at her plate, confused. She'd been dwarfed by this image she was sure they had of her, internalizing their perceptions, when it wasn't the truth.

And yet, it was.

She was different. A rebel in a family of well-behaved smart people. And she kind of liked it that way.

"I might want to do something in fashion. Maybe part-time, if I can swing it." She didn't look up, needing to get the words out before she lost her nerve. "The Maine College of Art offers a B.F.A., but there's also a continuing education program I could try, if you guys could help out with the cost."

A heavy pause followed. Jamie dragged her eyes up and was met with a knowing smile.

"I think we could swing that. Let's talk it over with your father this weekend."

She gave a gruff nod, thankful. A little weight had been lifted. They still had stuff to work through, but it was a step in the right direction.

"Eat," her mother said. "Your dinner's getting cold."

She tucked into her food. Her mother reached to the far end of the table and picked up an envelope Jamie immediately recognized.

"We never got to thank your friend Dean for the photographs," she said.

A ball of nerves wound themselves back into Jamie's stomach.

"I thanked him for us," she replied dryly. "No worries."

"Did you look at them?"

She shook her head. It hadn't been high on her priority list before their weekend, and it definitely wasn't now.

"There are a lot of pictures of you," her mother said. "Is there something to that?"

Meaning: was there something going on between her and Dean?

Easy answer. "No."

"Okay. You might want to see them anyway. I'll leave them here for you." She stood and kissed the top of Jamie's head. "I'm going to take a bath."

She called out a thank you to her mother's retreating form and finished her dinner, shooting wary glances at the packet in between bites. It stared silently back at her.

Curiosity took over. Jamie wiped her hands off and peeled the flap open.

The photos weren't professional, but they were obviously good, some even strikingly so. Artful perspectives of the ceremony site. Beautiful moments caught of the bride and groom. It brought a reluctant smile to her lips, and a healthy dose of heartache.

So unfair, that he'd thrown this talent away.

She flipped past several pictures of her—with the bridal party, on the dance floor, but there were no more of her than there were of anyone else. Jamie thought her mother might have gone a little bit loopy until she came to the last photo.

It was of her, standing to the side during the cake cutting, Kim and Sean in the background. Her shoulders didn't look abnormally large and her hair was actually behaving for once. Somehow, he'd made her look amazing, but it wasn't her appearance that shocked her.

The bride and groom should've been the ones in the spotlight, and yet Dean had been focused on her.

She dropped the photo in disgust, her dinner forming a sickening weight in her stomach. He could see her like this, could find the right light and perspective when he was behind the lens, the right touch when they were under the sheets, but he couldn't make an actual commitment. He couldn't step up to the fucking plate, not when it came to something real. Everything he'd said about her being a bright spot of sunshine in his life, about her being his favorite—they were all lines he fed her. All part of the games they played. She'd waited for him for six years, and in the end, she was nothing more than a pretty picture to him.

She was done waiting.

Placing the photos back in the envelope, Jamie went up to her room and booted up her laptop. She had a future to start thinking about, a life to get on with, and she was ready to figure it out.

TWELVE

Dean called in sick to work on Saturday, not wanting to deal with anything, the garage included. He'd spent the day home instead, holed up on his couch in front of the TV.

He hadn't spoken to Jamie all week. It was killing him, but he knew he'd done the right thing. She'd given up on the exciting life she'd always wanted because it would've meant not being near him, and that was unacceptable.

She didn't actually want him, anyway. Not the real him, not in the light of day, in a life where medical school and country clubs were the norm. She wanted Dean Trescott, Player Extraordinaire. And even if she thought he was what she wanted right now? Ten, twenty years down the line, she'd realize the mistake she'd made. She'd end up hating him, just like his old man and his mom.

She'd be fine. She said as much on Sunday, when she told him they were good. He could tell she was pissed—there was a definite bite to her voice when she'd said it—but he knew she'd get over it. Jamie bounced back, like those springy curls of hers, returning to their original shape after they'd been pulled too tight.

He was bouncing back to his old ways too. Or at least he was trying.

He'd hit the bar circuit several times this week. He'd met some women, exchanged numbers with a few and promised to call, but he wasn't feeling the scene. He came home and worked out instead, pounding out as many pull-ups as he could handle, then hit the floor for push-ups until he was about to pass out. It didn't take the edge off the way a good hard fucking would have, but for the first time in as long as he could remember, the idea of taking someone new to bed felt like too much energy.

He didn't want to have to put on the charm. He wanted to be around someone who knew him.

He wanted Jamie. And he didn't have a fucking clue what to do with that.

Maybe it hadn't been a good idea to go away in the first place, but he'd wanted one chance to be with her, to bask in the brightness of her smile. He'd lunged for it knowing the clock was ticking, needing to memorize what she felt like. Tasted like. One chance to pretend at the life he could've had if things were different.

That he could be more than he was.

But things weren't different, and wanting more wasn't in the cards for him, with work or with Jamie. He'd branded that reminder onto his chest years ago.

He shut the TV off and sighed. Too restless to sit around any longer, he reached for his phone. Mikey had been oddly MIA for once, so he shot Connor a text to meet him at their old haunt by the river.

Throwing on some clothes, he trekked out to his truck and drove to the Stroudwater neighborhood, parking by the stretch of land where Congress Street overlooked the Fore River. Back in their early days of misbehaving, he and Connor used to sneak down here, underage and hiding a six-pack between them in the darkened shadows of the marshland.

Padding beneath the overpass, Dean sought out a dry stretch of grass and plunked down ass-first onto the ground. The sky was cloudy, as somber as his mood. On the opposite side of the water, more leaves had scattered on the ground than remained behind on the tree limbs, peak foliage time having come and gone. Squirrels were scurrying through the brush, collecting supplies for the impending winter.

Maslow's Hierarchy was everywhere, even right there in nature. Trees and animals lived off what they needed, never aspiring for more, surviving each season, powering on through the next. He'd managed that way for years, taking each day as it came, and it had suited him just fine.

It really sucked that it wasn't working right now.

He'd be able to shake it off. It would just take time.

The buzzing sound of a motorcycle ended in a low rumble. Dean heard the heavy thump of feet meeting land when Connor hopped over the guardrail.

"Somebody die, or did you run out of condoms?" he asked.

"Funny."

Connor smiled like a guy who was getting it regularly, and with someone he really cared about. Dean always thought he was the comic relief in their group. The role reversal pissed him off.

"You look like shit, so I figured it had to be one or the other." Connor dropped to the ground and stretched his Incredible Hulk-sized legs out toward the water. "So, what's up?"

Dean shook his head. He wanted company, not a fucking shoulder to cry on. What was next if he did that? Braiding each other's hair?

"Nothing. Just bored," he said. "You?"

"I'm selling my bike."

"What?" Dean sputtered. Connor loved that stupid thing. He'd rebuilt it with his own hands at the shop he used to work at before he'd gone all technophile and left that life behind him. "Why?"

"I'm saving up to buy Gabby a ring."

Dean's mouth fell open. "You can't be serious."

He didn't mean to sound like a dick, but they'd only been together since July. How was the guy ready to make that kind of a commitment?

Connor didn't seem the slightest bit fazed. "Dead serious. Why?"

Dean ripped a few ragged strands of grass and tossed them into the river.

"Seems kind of fast," he said. "Not to mention that the bike is your only set of wheels. How are you planning on getting around?"

"I figure I'll ask your sorry ass for rides."

Dean snorted out a laugh. "Don't count on it."

Connor flipped him the bird and grinned.

"I can trade it in for a cheaper model if I want. My old boss is gonna work something out for me. And my grandparents might let me borrow their car for a while." He shrugged and looked up at the sky. "I'll work it out. It's not important. Only Gabby is."

Dean tore more shards of wasted grass from the ground. They landed in the water, causing a tiny ripple in the flat calm. It didn't ebb or flow, no progress forward, like everything in his world had been for the last six years.

"How do you know?" he asked quietly.

"Know what?"

"That it's right with her."

Connor sat forward and balanced his elbows on his knees.

"The bike's just a thing. Something I can save up for and buy again. Gabby is much more than that." His buddy looked over at him, that same contented look on his face he'd had since the summer ended, the one that erased the angry grimace of the rebellious kid he'd once been. "So is Jamie."

Dean tensed. He started to blow it off, but couldn't come up with a damn thing.

"Look, it's none of my business," Connor said. "And you can go on pretending if you want, but you guys have been like two sides of the same coin since the tenth grade."

It was true, but it didn't matter. Dean shook his head. "I'm no good for her, man. I'll ruin her life. She's better off without me."

"Right. Don't try for anything at all, and you'll be happy."

"Fuck off."

Connor laughed. "You know, I was listening that day in detention when we learned about the Hierarchy of Needs, and you got it all wrong. It's not that we shouldn't shoot for more. It's the opposite. Everyone deserves to have what they want, Dean. Not scrape by on what they think they need."

Everyone deserves to have what they want.

Sure. He'd just wave a magic wand and make that happen.

Connor clapped a hand on his shoulder, a silent communication. Dean nodded mutely, still staring out at the water as Connor gathered himself up, kicked his bike into gear and rode off into the distance.

Dean stayed until the sky grew dark and his ass was going numb from sitting on the cold ground. He started his truck, but found himself heading south instead of home, past the Jetport and to the old house he grew up in.

He parked in front of the cracked sidewalk, his jaw nearly soldered shut at the sight of peeling blue siding and faded brown shutters, leaves unceremoniously dumped into sagging brown bags by the curb. The front yard he'd once played in was overgrown, and the S in the family name had broken off the label on the mailbox. He had no idea what he was doing here—he'd avoided this place as much as possible since he moved out—but something kept him from driving away.

The TV flickered through the living room windows. The old man was home.

Dean cut the engine, made his way up the broken cement and let himself in. The interior hadn't changed since his mother left: the same dilapidated cabinets in the kitchen, the same crusty stove. He'd bet his room in the attic had remained unchanged too, unless his father was using it to store more of the crap he could never throw out.

He didn't want to go upstairs to check.

"Guess you're feeling better." His father's gruff sarcasm carried over the sound of a Boston College football game on the living room TV. "There's beer in the fridge, if you want it."

"Thanks, I'm good."

Dean trudged across the creaking floorboards and sank onto the couch. His father was still in work clothes, a rotation of dirty slacks and long-sleeved shirts that never varied, no matter what the season. Dean wasn't so different, each day spent in his uniform of jeans, boots and a Henley tee.

He was turning into the old man already.

It never bothered him before, back when he'd first drunk the Kool-Aid of the family business. When he'd thought the name Trescott was something to be proud of. Things had changed, and he'd stepped forward to the chopping block regardless, accepting the fact that one day his father's daily existence would become his own. That eventuality had seemed years off, but Dean had spent the whole day in the same position as the one Chuck was in right now.

Was this the only life he could ever hope to have? To spend his Saturday nights sitting in a broken-down house, drinking beers and watching a game alone?

The idea made him genuinely feel sick.

His father hadn't been concerned over why Dean had called in today, either. He was just annoyed that his assistant manager hadn't put in his time. It didn't matter if a cog in the wheel wasn't feeling well, only that it worked right.

What the hell was he doing this for?

Dean looked at his father. "Why do you want me to take over the shop?"

The old man's gaze never strayed from the television. "Because people trust businesses that are family-owned, especially ones run by a second or third generation."

All the emotion Dean had kept under wraps pushed up against a dam inside him. Overflow was imminent.

"Customer trust gets built up over years," his father continued. "It'll do even better with you."

Dean's stomach churned. The anger rolling through him was like spitfire, his father's reply a shot of gasoline. The legacy Dean was being handed was never about *him*. It was what *he* could do for the business. A business he wouldn't be allowed to make any changes in until his father had gotten them so deep in the red that Dean would never be able to pull them out of it.

He was through with being tied to that future, dragged toward it by a freight train he couldn't direct.

He didn't want that life anymore.

"I quit."

His father's gaze slid slowly over and landed on him. "What the hell do you mean, you quit?"

"I mean exactly what it sounds like. I quit."

"You can't *quit*. This is what we do. The shop is for you."

"It's not for me!" Dean shot up off the couch, his rage hitting a boiling point. "It's so I can fix the mess you've made. You expect me to sit here and take orders, to watch you run the place into the ground, and I won't do it anymore. The business is falling apart, and I'm not sticking around just to inherit an albatross."

His words stung. Dean could see it in the way his father's eyes burned.

"I kept the business alive to give to you," the old man growled.

"It's not alive. It's barely breathing. You think you built it up to give to me, but there won't be anything left if it goes down the tubes."

Dean had the advantage in height, but his father's glare still had the power to level him. He held his ground.

"You can't walk away from your heritage," he said. "It's in your blood. Running this shop is what you've always wanted."

"It's not what I want," Dean spat back. "Since when have you given a damn about what I want? You never even asked."

They stayed silent and stared at each other across the bare floorboards, battleships poised on edge, each waiting for the other to strike. The sharp whistles and cheers of the game was the only sound until his father swallowed, a small move of resignation.

"All right," he said. "Tell me what you want."

Dean couldn't reply at first. The ability to fill in that blank was a liberty he didn't know what to do with.

"I don't want to quit," he said quietly. "But I won't stay on if you don't start letting me make real changes."

Another beat of silence. "What kind of changes?"

Dean sat back down on the couch. It was strange, to have his father's complete attention. To feel like a grown-up around him, for once.

"First, we've got to start working with the insurance companies. It doesn't matter how low we make our prices. If we're not on the adjusters' lists, people won't find us."

He didn't hit the usual resistance with that idea, so he kept going.

"I know it means negotiating lower labor and material rates to get repair contracts, but we can still be the good guys. If a rep tells us to put an aftermarket part on a car that's barely a year old, we tell the customer. Yeah, we run the risk of being taken off that company's list, but we'll have made a connection with the client. We'll still be building trust."

His father looked at the wall. Looked back. "All right," he said. "What else?"

Energy started pulsing through him. "We've got to get computerized. Either paying for QuickBooks or hiring that virtual bookkeeper," Dean said. "Also, I want you to look at this workflow software I found. It puts the production schedule in one place, and even updates the customers through email or text message every time we finish a task."

His father ran his fingers over the bristles on his chin. The slant of his eyebrows suggested he actually seemed interested.

"Anything else?"

He took a deep breath. Jamie's suggestion had idled in the back of his brain all week. He'd poked through the *Want-Ad Digest* and found at least a dozen classic cars for sale, ones that could be fixed up without too much cost.

Dean wanted it to be possible—the idea that they could give something new a shot.

He stood up. Paced around the room. Stared at the floor and rubbed his hand over the back of his head.

"I want to discuss adding restoration as a new arm of the business," he said.

No reply. Dean continued to pace.

"I know what you're going to say, but we need to offer something that will set us apart. The only way we're going to survive is by doing things the chains can't, and this is it. You can't take your 1932 Ford Model-B Roadster to Walmart for a cleanup. You've got to bring it to someone who knows how to tune those parts, and that's us. We can't compete on price, but *this*...this we can do."

The silence was deafening. Dean couldn't take it any longer. He dragged his eyes up.

His father had his chin lifted, and was regarding Dean with an expression that looked like respect.

"This is why I knew I was doing the right thing in planning to hand the business down to you," he said. "Because you'll run it better than I ever have."

It was the closest he'd ever come to saying he was proud of him.

They talked for a while longer, a new kind of accord between them as they hashed out ideas. It was after midnight by the time Dean finally got back home, but it could've been noon for how charged up he was. The future in front of him didn't feel like a dead end anymore. It felt like an open road.

And the first person he wanted to tell was Jamie.

But she wasn't his to tell, wasn't his to call in the middle of the night and share good news. The reality of how things were between them punched a hole right through him.

Dean went into his bedroom and looked at his camera bag. It was sitting in the corner, where he'd dumped it when he got home on Sunday. All the photos from the weekend were still on it —the cars and Jamie at the fair.

Her body, gorgeous and naked in their hotel room.

She inspired him, not just as a stunning subject to be photographed, but in life too. He never would've summoned the guts to talk to his father about all this if it weren't for her.

How many things would he never have tried for, if it weren't in the pursuit of her smile?

He probably would've walked straight out of that art class and never looked back.

Moving on instinct, Dean went to his closet and gingerly extracted his portfolio. Sitting on the edge of his bed, he balanced it on his lap, taking a minute to finger its rich, grained texture. Then he dragged the zipper around the sides until it fell open.

One by one, he paged through the plastic sleeves, looking at his work. A black-and-white shot of the tree line by the high school baseball field. A self portrait he'd taken in the side-view mirror of his truck. A close-up of a shiny bumper from when he'd experimented with macro. Gray waves freezing as they crossed over the sand one extremely cold day in winter. They were all moments that had struck him in some way, ones he had to find ways to capture.

Like when he'd photographed Jamie at the wedding.

The same feeling that hit him like a club that day sucked the air out of his lungs again, but Dean realized there was more to it than a desire to claim her. What he really wanted was to be on the other side of the lens, her hand warm in his, a heavy piece of silverware between them as they sliced through their own wedding cake.

He wanted a future with her. To have her in his bed every morning, wake up to her smile and know it was for him. To clean gutters in their first house and jump in leaf piles they'd spent hours raking. To see all the ways she could figure out how to dress a belly swollen with his child.

He'd been in love with her his whole goddamn life. She was his best friend, not to mention the best sex he'd ever had. She *knew* him in a way no one else did, but he'd pushed her away over and over again because he wanted her to find someone on her level.

He'd never entertained the idea that he could actually be that someone.

She had, though. She'd given him so many opportunities to see that over the years, but he'd been too mired in his own crap to realize it. He thought he was protecting her, shielding her from the only future he could offer her, but that future was changing now.

He was changing into the man he wanted to be.

Dean closed the portfolio, went back to his closet and rifled through the hangers. He'd spent a lifetime not going after what he wanted, telling himself to be content with the status quo. But he deserved a better life than the one he was living.

And he didn't want to live without her in it anymore.

THIRTEEN

Jamie pushed through the doors of the community center and blinked in the brilliant wash of midday sun. The weekly Sunday farmer's market was set up on the street, the cobblestones alive with tables and tents. Harvest vegetables made squat piles on bales of straw, the air laced with the scents of apple cider and cinnamon. Some of her students waved from the crowd. She waved back happily and breathed in deep.

A massive weight had been lifted. She'd turned down the assistant director job.

Her boss had been disappointed, but Jamie explained it would've taken her out of the water too much. Being in the pool, teaching kids how to achieve, and eventually, surpass her skill level—that was where she belonged.

She hadn't wanted to commit herself to the position either, when there were some possible changes coming up in her future.

Zipping up her parka, Jamie nearly skipped toward her car. She hadn't needed the aid of an outfit this morning to bolster her courage. Her high-heeled boots, dark slacks, gray ruffled shirt and matching sparkly scarf just made her feel good—clothes that reflected how confident she was on the inside now.

The change made her smile.

Her grin sagged when she reached the parking lot. Dean was in the front row, leaning against the grill of his truck, one foot hiked up on the bumper behind him. He stood up when he saw her and squinted in the sunlight, his hair turned to gold in its rays.

Jamie's legs went numb. She couldn't seem to move from the curb.

"What are you doing here?"

He opened his mouth. Closed it again. Looked at the ground and laughed. "I wanted to talk to you."

Talk. A funny thing to want to do when this time last week he was breaking her heart.

"How'd you know where I was?"

Dean laughed again and rubbed the back of his neck with his palm. "I kind of...went to your house and asked your mom."

He lifted his gaze to hers and offered her a sheepish grin. The half smile was an ice pick to her sternum.

He'd probably run out of women to call and was hoping for a quick hit. Or maybe he wanted to see if she'd be willing to make a habit out of last weekend's events. Pencil her in for one day a week on his constantly rotating calendar. Whatever he was here for, she didn't care. She wasn't riding that roller coaster again.

"We have nothing to talk about, Dean. Go home."

She strode past him, and was halfway past his truck when he called out, "I thought you said we were good."

The words nailed her to the spot. Jamie's blood ran cold.

"I lied," she barked, her hands clenching into fists as she whipped around to face him. Dean took a half step backward. "Don't look so shocked. Did you really think we were okay after that?"

It took him a minute to find his voice. "No," he admitted. "I just...hoped we were."

"Why?" she asked, then thought better of it. "You know what? It doesn't matter what you say, because I know all you're going to do is walk away again. It's all you *ever* do. You don't actually care."

Dean pinched his brows together in confusion, little wrinkles imprinted between them.

"Of course I care," he uttered softly. "More than you know."

"That's such bullshit."

"It's not," he said. "I can't walk away. I never could. I just knew I wasn't right for you."

Jamie narrowed her eyes, all her muscles tense. "What the hell is that supposed to mean?"

He sighed and shook his head.

"I've never fit into your world, Jamie. You're beautiful and talented and you've got the whole world in front of you, and me —" He cut off his words with a shrug. "I've been some grease monkey. Nothing more than a small-time mechanic."

Hurt and anger welled up inside her. "I've never thought of you that way. Not once. I can't believe you'd think that I would."

"I know you don't." He moved toward her, then inched back, hesitant. "*I* thought of me that way. That's why I acted the way I did. I wanted you to find someone else. Someone who was worthy of you."

"So you put me on some kind of pedestal?" She stepped back to him, close enough to hiss, "Someone you could fuck, but never actually be with?"

He recoiled slightly. "That's not true."

It was. She'd seen the proof of it, in a glossy four-by-six on her kitchen table.

"It is, Dean. This has never been about anything more than sex to you. You've made that pretty damn clear."

She started to move away, but he followed after her.

"Jamie, please. I never meant to hurt you. I just didn't want this life for you."

"What *life*?"

"The only one I could've offered you. One that was never going to be anything more than bargain basements and cutting coupons."

She gaped at him, so frustrated she could've torn her hair out. "So you made the choice for me?" she shouted. "What gives you the right to do that?"

"I thought—" He sighed again and kicked at the ground. "I thought it was the right thing to do. That eventually you'd figure out you didn't belong here and move on."

He was waiting for her to figure things out, just like her parents. Except for Dean, it was only a method for pushing her away.

Years of wounded pride bubbled to the surface. She pointed a finger at him.

"You don't get to decide my fate for me, Dean. You can't tell me what kind of life to have, where I should live it or who I should spend it with. I can make those decisions for myself."

He started to talk, but Jamie spoke over him, because she was done listening.

"At least I tried with what I wanted. At least I gave it a shot. You threw your hands in the air and gave up. That's the only difference between us. Any others were all in your head. But if you can't see that, then I have nothing more to say to you."

Jamie spun around and stomped away, rifling through her purse for her keys.

"You're right," Dean called out, but she kept walking. "You always have been. I see that now. And that's why I quit."

She stopped her in her tracks and turned around slowly. "You quit your father's garage?"

"I did," he said with a shrug. "Well, quit and then agreed to come back with conditions."

He stood up a little taller when he said it too. He crossed the pavement to meet her and moved in close. Too close for her to think properly.

"Have a cup of coffee with me," he said. "And I'll explain everything."

Jamie eyed him warily. A different Dean was standing in front of her. It took her a second to realize he was out of his usual uniform, his jeans and Henley traded for a leather jacket and khakis, shoes instead of boots. He didn't look like he was hiding though, or trying to be someone else. The collar of his shirt was low enough to reveal a taste of ink, that perpetual scruff forming a fine line over his jaw.

His clothes, his demeanor—it was like he'd shed a skin, and then grown into himself, somehow.

"Since when do you drink coffee instead of beer?" she asked.

Dean chuckled softly. "Since I started trying to do things right."

Jamie wasn't ready to trust him yet, but his eyes pleaded with hers, and this new version of him was too intriguing for her not to at least hear him out.

They walked to the coffee shop on the corner, ordered drinks and found a table by the window. Their spoons made music against the ceramic cups, a thick silence in the air between them.

"I suck at this," he said.

"You do," she replied matter-of-factly "You're used to women throwing themselves at you."

Nervous laughter was followed by him rapping his knuckles against the table. He was uncomfortable, but she liked seeing him like this, some of that suave exterior flayed away.

"I did try, you know," he said. "With the whole college and

photography thing. But when my dad said he needed me in the business, I knew that was it for school, and for...us."

He looked up at her. Green eyes glittered.

"It was right after our night by the cove when he told me that," he said.

Some of the anger Jamie had been harboring melted into regret—sadness for the teenager who'd been so excited over a possible future, only to have it dashed before his eyes.

"That's why you said it was a mistake."

He nodded. "I didn't want to hold you back."

One by one, the pieces started falling into place. The words "we still good" had never been a dismissal. They were his way of checking on her, of making sure she'd stay in his life in some small way even when he wanted her to find someone else.

"Explain that picture you took at the wedding," she said. "The one of me by the cake."

Dean sighed. "You were gorgeous that day. I almost couldn't concentrate on anything else. But I felt like, the way my life was, I could never be more for you than the hired help. The guy who got you out of a bind."

The idea made her heart hurt. He didn't see himself the way she did—the artist beneath the gruff exterior, the playboy with the beautiful soul inside. She reached over, tentative at first, then took his hand in hers and threaded their fingers together.

"You've never been that guy to me."

"I know." He squeezed her hand and gave her a small smile, one that lit her up from the inside out. "You've always believed in me. Now I've got to believe in myself. I don't want to be that guy anymore, which is why I told my dad I was quitting, unless he agreed to let me change things."

"And he's going to?"

"Yes. Everything we talked about in New Hampshire and more." Dean's excitement was tangible.

"That's amazing," Jamie said. "I'm so proud of you."

He beamed, then looked down at their joined hands.

"I knew you would be," he said softly. He ran his thumb over her knuckles, then swallowed and inhaled a shaky breath as his eyes found hers again. "I've been an idiot, pushing you away. I should've said this sooner, but you have to know it's not just sex with you, and never has been, because I love you."

She blinked. "What?"

"I love you," he repeated. "I have since I was sixteen years old. And all I want out of life is to find some way to make my family's business succeed, take some pictures and wake up next to you every day until I'm a hundred."

Jamie couldn't reply at first, her emotions so thoroughly tangled she couldn't tell what she was feeling. She opened her mouth, hoping she could find the right words, but he stopped her with a shake of his head.

"Don't say anything yet. Let me finish."

She nodded, and then Dean's face darkened. His brows pressed low, lips pinching to a thin line.

"I can't offer you much now. I think down the line I can, but Jamie, I meant it when I said you deserved an amazing life. I know you wanted to be in New York, and if I'm the reason you never—" His words dropped off. He cleared his throat. "My parents broke up because my mom got stuck here. No matter how I feel about you, I don't want you to stay here for me. You'll end up hating me, and I couldn't live with that."

There was so much hurt in his eyes. So much insecurity and fear. Jamie had always combated those kinds of emotions with humor. She waved a casual hand in the air.

"Don't flatter yourself. I already made my decision. I'm not sticking around Portland for you."

He drew in an unsteady breath. "So you are leaving, then."

She paused for a moment, just to mess with him, then said,

"Nah. I actually kinda like it here, and there's a fashion design program at the Maine College of Art I've been thinking of applying to. I'm going to give that a shot."

His eyes went wide, that childlike hope she hadn't seen in years shining out of them.

"That would make you happy?"

"Yes. I can go part-time if I get in and keep my job at the center too, because I don't want to give up swimming either. I'm pretty good at it." She shrugged and grinned, folding her other hand around both of theirs. "The best of both worlds, without the expensive Manhattan rent."

He laughed and leaned toward her until their shoulders touched. Jamie studied their entwined hands, the curls of ink peeking out from under his sleeve.

"I wish you'd told me sooner," she said.

"Told you what?"

"That you love me." She took a breath. It was a heavy moment, one that definitely required more air. "Maybe if you'd told me the way you felt, it wouldn't have taken me so long for me to figure out that I love you too."

All the tension rushed out of him, the sheer emotion in his eyes making full impact on Jamie's chest. She had more to say though, more he needed to hear about how she truly felt, so she kept talking.

"You're the person I've compared everyone else to over the years. The reason I ended every relationship I've been in. And it wouldn't have mattered to me if you were a mechanic or a photographer or a doctor."

Dean closed his eyes and bowed his head.

"I've always belonged to you," she said, her voice cracking. "Since that night in your truck, I've been yours."

He lifted his head on an exhale and kissed her. It wasn't rough or hard, not fueled by desperation or lust. It was soft and sweet, a tender brush of lips, a stroke of his mouth over hers that soothed all the scars of the past six years.

Dean pulled back and pressed his forehead to hers. "Say it again."

"Say what."

"That you love me."

Jamie smiled. Brought her lips to his ear. Whispered, "I love you" and chased her teeth along his earlobe. Dean shivered, wove his free hand into her hair and kissed her again. The tug of his fingers and quick slip of his tongue against hers stole her breath.

Panting, she peeked over his shoulder to make sure no one was listening, then gave him a sultry look from beneath lowered lashes. "I don't want you making decisions for me again, okay? There's only one place I want you doing that."

His eyes blazed. A low groan sounded in his throat.

"Not in my life," she said. "Just in your bed."

He pulled her hair a little harder. Jamie's eyes drooped shut. When she opened them, his gaze was fiercely trained on her. Still watching her, still taking her in.

"What is it with you and watching me?"

Dean half laughed, half winced. He let go of her hair and ducked his head down, cheeks coloring.

"Are you actually blushing?"

He exhaled hard. Embarrassed Dean was like a meteor shower—rare and easily missed if you didn't catch it quickly enough. She nudged him until he lifted his head. His cheek was curved up to one side, the playboy smirk erased by a bashful smile she'd never seen before.

"I'm kind of a reaction junkie," he said. "The sights and sounds of pleasure...I get off on it."

"No wonder you were always such a good photographer. You like to watch."

He grunted. It was a fingernail snagged on something. A caught nerve.

"What?" she asked.

"Watching you. It's been my longest-running fantasy. Ever since you showed up in detention dressed as an angel."

An empty ache grew and pulsed inside her. "Really?"

Now it was his turn to lean in close, his grin wicked. "You have no idea how many times I've thought about watching you get yourself off in those sparkly wings. That halo."

Jamie bit her lip. She wanted him somewhere private. Wanted him securing her wrists above her head and fucking her, hard and fast. Overpowering her. Consuming her.

"It was never about the costume, though," he said.

She was almost disappointed. "No kinky role-playing for you?"

Dean's smile gentled. "No. It's because I saw you that day. The real you. Angel face. Bad kid underneath. Wild. Free." He kissed her. "You."

Tears sparked in her eyes. Her heart skipped a beat. He saw her. He'd *always* seen her. Better than anyone else ever had.

They finished their drinks, and he put his arm around her as they made their way down the street. It wasn't an absent-minded touch, or a movement made out of drunken playfulness. It was purposeful, intentional. One that told everyone who walked past them that she was his.

The sun was starting its descent when they reached the parking lot, the air growing chilly and crisp. Jamie huddled close to him and placed her palm on his chest, a gentle touch above the etched-out stars over his heart.

The meaning of his other tattoos had come to her easily. This one was still a mystery.

"What do the stars mean?"

He covered her hand with his. Blond lashes drifted low. "They were a reminder."

"Of?"

His eyes met hers. "To stay away from love."

"With me, or anyone?"

"Both," he said. "Mostly you."

She pursed her lips, mouth twisting to the side. Dean pecked her with light kisses until she giggled.

"I put the stars here to remind myself that I couldn't offer anyone a future. That it was better not to love anyone at all." He spread her hand out, a light touch to each fingertip. "I didn't want to need love. Because then I could lose it."

She shot him a wry grin. "So that's why you're such a player."

A hoarse laugh burst out of him. He played with the tips of her fingers. "Not anymore, I guess?"

It was a question and an offer. Jamie shook her head up at the sky and looked back at him again.

"Dean Trescott, off the market. Women are going to come after me with pitchforks."

He smiled. "So we're doing this? For real?"

She looked into those little-boy eyes, thinking of how much they had in common. How long they'd both been hurting, but pretending they were okay. Too scared to admit how they felt, afraid of the toll rejection would bring.

It was time to put that behind them.

She wrapped her arms around his waist and kissed him.

"Yeah," she said. "We are."

FOURTEEN

Dean hauled another pile of junk into the bin in the parking lot. It landed on top of the pile with a gratifying clatter. It had to have been the thirtieth time he'd done that today—his back ached and his hands were a mess—but every thud of metal against metal made him happier than he'd been in years.

He glanced out at the harbor. The red-brick buildings of downtown were lit with the orange flame of the sinking sun, the waterfront thatched with cloudy pockets of blue, pink and red. It was the kind of early evening that begged to be photographed, but there would be others.

Right now he had a more important task at hand.

He trudged back inside, wiping his brow with a dirty forearm as he stepped through the wide bay door. He'd sweat straight through his shirt, which was crazy considering the fact that it would be November in the morning. It was a good workout, though. A shower was definitely in order, but that was hours off.

Maybe not too many, though, considering the help he had.

Half the guys were over here today, clearing a path through everything stored on the first floor of the warehouse. His father was directing things, and Connor and Mikey had taken the day off work to help too. They'd split the place into sections: the far right was where they'd stacked body parts. Engine pieces in the middle. Boxes of files were up against the left wall, ready to be scanned and shredded.

Dean grinned at the concrete slab, visible for the first time in years. He'd been surprised to see there was actually a floor there, underneath all that stuff. Watching his father sort through things, it occurred to Dean why the old man had been such a packrat. It wasn't just about saving money. He'd held onto everything he could because he'd lost so much, and was terrified of losing anything else.

It was an emotion Dean could completely identify with.

Now both of them were ready to let go of the past, and a new future was shining out from that cement block, one Dean had never wanted to try for because he'd thought it was impossible.

Maybe reaching for the kind of life he wanted wasn't such a bad thing after all.

He bent over, gearing up to haul the next pile out to the Dumpster when he was suddenly attacked from behind. Arms and legs wrapped around him as something heavy smacked against his side, knocking the wind out of him.

Dean fell forward and caught himself on the wall. "What the hell, Matthews?"

Jamie dug her chin into his shoulder. "How'd you know it was me?"

"The chlorine smell. Gives you away every time."

She'd complained about constantly smelling like pool chemicals, but the scent didn't bother him. If anything, it reminded him how recently Jamie had been naked.

She stuck out her tongue, then nuzzled his cheek. "Sorry my bag hit you."

So that was what had careened into him. "What the hell do you have in there, anyway? A brick?"

"The November issue of *Vogue*."

He huffed out an amused breath through his nose. "You and your fashion obsession."

It wasn't an obsession anymore—it was the career she was trying for—but teasing her was his sole privilege, now that they were officially dating. He shifted her weight on his back.

"You know, if you weren't my favorite girl, I'd have dropped you on your ass by now."

Jamie giggled. "If you did that, then you wouldn't have anyone to go the Halloween party with tonight." She kissed his cheek, then hopped to the ground and pulled out a pamphlet. "I grabbed this for you today."

He glanced at what she was holding out, then held up his dirty hands and shook his head.

"Take it upstairs. I'll look at it later."

She grinned, that fantastic Jamie smile that was all his. A glittering hair band held back her wild curls. Curls he'd wrapped around his fist that morning when she'd woken him up with her mouth.

She'd slept in his bed nearly every night in the two weeks since their talk at the coffee shop. It had meant Mikey hadn't been taking up his usual place on his couch. Dean felt badly about it, but had a feeling his buddy understood. He and Jamie needed to make up for lost time.

They'd done more than make up for it, their nights filled with crazy nonstop sex. Several mornings too. They'd both been late for work more than a few times. He couldn't get enough. Against the wall in the living room. In the hallway. On the kitchen counter.

In the back of his truck under some blankets by the beach, because yeah, that needed to happen.

The life he'd been afraid wouldn't be good enough for her—nights at home and meals that subsisted mostly of PB and J and cereal—didn't seem to bother her either. She actually had a thing for junk food, although the hours she spent swimming and getting sweaty with him more than took care of burning off the calories. He was keeping the pounds off himself, now that he was working out daily and scaling back on the beer.

He didn't seem to need the booze anymore. Not when he was coming home to Jamie every night. She'd filled his world with life in so little time, and he was surprised how quickly he was ready to offer her what he'd never given anyone before.

It went beyond wanting to give her a key to his apartment, though. He was ready to let her decorate the place, to move in and make her energy a part of his world.

To let the world know he was taken.

Jamie tucked the information on the Maine College of Art's photography program into her bag and walked backwards to the door.

"See you up there when you're done," she said. "And don't forget to let me know when you're coming up. I don't want you to see the costumes until they're done."

"You're not finished with them yet?"

She'd been working on their Halloween outfits as a trial-run project, to see if she could sew something decent on her own. She'd been pretty hush-hush about them too, hiding them in a box she stashed in her car whenever he came home.

"Almost. Just be glad I still have all my fingers," she said merrily.

Oh, he was glad all right. He wanted every single one of those fingers clasping his when he made her come later tonight.

Dean went back to work, a big stupid grin on his face. He didn't care. Jamie was upstairs waiting for him, in the mini studio he'd created for her in an empty corner. He'd surprised her one morning by setting up a table in the space where the most light filtered in and telling her it was hers. Now that table was littered with dozens of charcoal pencils, her magazines in haphazard piles. She'd brought over an easel and propped a new sketchpad on it. The most recent additions were a mannequin torso she'd found at Goodwill and an antique sewing machine she'd bought off Craigslist.

She was happier than he'd ever seen her. It made him stand up tall, knowing he'd helped make that happen.

She was encouraging him to find his way back to the arts too, but Dean wasn't there yet. It was enough that she was putting together a new portfolio and applying to that fashion design program. She had no idea if it was going to work out, but she was taking a risk, and Dean was taking one with her.

Coming up with a plan on how to make the restoration thing a reality had been a challenge, but it was one he was more than ready for. He'd shown his father the photographs he'd taken at the fair, ready to prove that what he had in mind would cost them some in the beginning, but would be worth it in the end.

There'd been some grumbles, some doubts, even an argument or two, but they were on the same side now. Partners, for once.

He'd had Connor update the business website to say that Trescott Auto Body would be offering classic car refurbishment soon. The calls they'd already gotten seemed to have been enough to get his father fired up over the idea. Dean had caught him looking at that old photo of his grandfather, saying the most senior Trescott had always talked about fixing up an old Model T, and maybe they could do that someday.

They'd even played around with the idea of leasing a company vehicle down the line, so Dean could bring his truck up to show quality.

He was getting to call more of the shots in the garage too, and had finally gotten a glimpse at how hard this must've been for the old man all these years. Running a small local shop in a world of chains was no easy task.

That was another reason Dean was putting off the photography thing. He wanted it to be part of his life, but the idea of going back to school for a degree in business was a lot more exciting. He didn't know how soon, but that was okay. What mattered now was that doing *more* suddenly felt possible.

Photography was something he could do in his downtime, and he'd started taking pictures whenever the moment struck him. The skyline outside his window at sunrise. Portland's downtown sidewalk at dusk, alive with people.

Racy ones of Jamie.

The memory made him want to abandon everything he was doing, go upstairs and tackle her, right the fuck now. But she wasn't going anywhere. The fears and worries about her moving on had all been him, a reflection of his upbringing, and that was a conversation he'd had to tackle too.

He'd needed to talk to his mother.

Calling her shouldn't have taken as much effort as it did. After all, she tried to show she still cared through her elaborate gifts. If it weren't for that camera, Dean wouldn't be where he was today. But there were things that needed to be said, so he'd gotten her on the phone for a heart-to-heart.

The conversation had been strained at first, because how exactly did you start things out with small talk before explaining to the woman who gave birth to you that her actions turned him into a man who was terrified of commitment?

He'd finally ripped the Band-Aid off and asked, point blank:

"Why didn't you stick around? Didn't you love Dad?"

"Didn't you love me?"

She took it all in, and was so quiet for a few moments Dean was sure she'd hung up on him, severing their ties for good. She finally answered that love wasn't the problem. Of course she loved him, and was sorry he even had to ask. She'd left because it was time, and she thought Dean had been old enough to handle it, and if she hadn't loved his father, she wouldn't have fought it out with him for so long. They simply grew apart, like so many people who fell for their best friend from high school and needed to move on.

He hung up, knowing nothing had actually changed between them, but that hadn't been the reason for his call. He'd needed to face head-on the reason he'd pushed Jamie away all these years: the idea that he'd play out his parents' lives, and by virtue of that, ruin hers.

He knew it was possible the same thing could happen for him and Jamie. They might eventually grow apart, but he wasn't going to let that stop him anymore. He couldn't, because the fact that he loved her was something he'd etched onto his skin years ago.

He'd punched black stars out over his heart as a reminder not to fall in love, but it had been about her all along. Stars shine in darkness, giving hope of a new, better path. Her star was imprinted on him because he'd been drawn to her, to the way she sparkled.

Jamie was the North Star missing from his compass.

It was long past sunset by the time he and the guys finished for the day. Dean thanked everyone for coming, got a good, firm handshake from his father and some fist bumps from Connor and Mikey. He took the stairs two at a time to the second floor, forgetting to text Jamie in his eagerness to be near her.

"Hey!" She shut off the sewing machine and stood in front of it. White, frilly fabric peeked out from behind her. "You were supposed to let me know you were on your way up."

He threw his hands up in surrender. "Sorry, sorry."

"You should be." The pout on her face was ridiculously adorable. He wanted to kiss it off her.

"Can I least have a preview of what I'll be wearing tonight?" he asked.

She scampered toward him and retrieved her phone from her pocket. "Fine. I'll show you the photo I got the inspiration from."

Dean looked at her instead of the screen, at the liveliness radiating from her. She'd shocked him last week by saying she was interested in getting a tattoo, and they'd stayed up late looking at pictures. She got all excited over one of a phoenix—a black body with wings the color of flame. She liked the idea of putting it on her lower back, saying the design symbolized her rising up from her own ashes. Starting over again.

He liked the idea of it being on a place on her body only he would see.

"Here." She held up a photo of a girl in a tutu and a tiara kissing a guy dressed as—

"Is he supposed to be the Tooth Fairy?"

She giggled. Dean shook his head.

"Oh no. You're not parading me around in a giant pillow and a crown. I'm not doing it."

She had him pretty damn whipped, but he had to draw the line somewhere.

Jamie rolled her eyes. "Relax. I said it was my inspiration. Not what I actually made."

The eye roll was almost as cute as her pout. He moved to put his arms around her, but she scurried back and pointed in the direction of the bathroom.

"Don't even think of touching me until you've showered."

Dean chuckled and did as he was told. He enjoyed her bossy side, and had gotten to see it in full force when he'd watched her coach one night. She was a fireball out there, and Dean had a feeling her renewed enthusiasm was a direct result of her turning down that promotion. She'd become more passionate in her pep talks, and the kids responded to her, taking longer strides in the water at her encouragement, attacking the water more vigorously when she clapped and shouted.

She seemed to have finally found some meaning in what she was doing—fulfillment in propelling her students toward exciting futures of their own.

He'd asked her to put the swimsuit and whistle back on when he'd gotten her home that night, and let her bark out some commands for him. It was a night he'd been glad to live in a commercial district, any neighbors too far away to hear them.

She was no longer in the living room when Dean reemerged in a towel, the day's grime washed away.

"I'm in the bedroom," she called out. "My costume's finished."

He followed the sound of her voice, stopping short at the entrance.

Tiny white dress. Frills that clung to her hips, barely covering her ass. White thigh-highs and matching heels. Shiny wings and a halo.

Dean swallowed. "You made that?"

"I did. I found the pattern online after that picture gave me the idea." She twirled around. "Guess I don't suck with a needle and thread after all."

She needed to stop talking about sucking. Not if she wanted to avoid ruining her costume.

She slipped out of her shoes, crawled onto his bed and sat back on her heels. "You like?"

He nodded gruffly. The ability to speak had escaped him.

"I thought you might." She stroked one toned thigh. Her fingers danced toward her panty line. "Since it's been your fantasy for so long."

Just like that, the fuse that never seemed to die out blazed into flame.

She crooked her other finger at him, beckoning him to the bed as she leaned back and spread her legs. Dean dropped the towel and staggered toward her. Mind blitzed. Body on overdrive. Her hand snaked beneath white satin panties. One slow circle of her finger over her clit and he groaned.

"Do it," he growled. "Let me see."

Jamie grinned, lush curls spread out over his pillows, the dirtiest angel imaginable. Dean sat down next to her, never taking his eyes away from what she was doing. He was hard in an instant, his dick stiff and begging for attention. Jamie reached for his hand with her free one and brought it to her mouth, tongue gliding along his palm.

"Show me," she said in between licks. "Show me what you'd do when you thought about me like this."

Dean cursed and wrapped his now-wet fingers around his cock. His hips rocked forward in time with hers, and he fought against the urge to take her as his dick slid into the tight circle of his fist. She'd orchestrated this for him, and the grandest gesture he could make right now was to watch her every move and show her how damn much he liked it.

"Is the live show as good as the fantasy?" Jamie asked, breathless.

"Better."

It was better than he'd ever dreamed. She was his sin and his salvation, all wrapped up in one pretty little package, moaning softly on his bed. She arched, jostling the halo, and something about seeing her all disheveled made it that much hotter.

He wasn't going to last long. And apparently, neither was she. Her breathing skipped to that pattern of rapid, shuddery inhales.

"Keep looking at me," she begged. "Love it when you stare at me like that."

"Love watching you," he said, his voice gravelly. "Sexiest goddamn thing I've ever seen."

Her free hand shot back to clutch the pillow behind her. "Dean—"

Her release seemed to split her in two, a powerful force that brought him there too, and Dean grabbed the towel before he made a mess of both of them.

Catching her breath, Jamie sat up and kissed his neck, a long, hot slip of her mouth on the column of his throat. He hissed when she scraped her teeth over the spot she knew he liked.

"All right," he said. "If you've got that on, then what's my costume? The devil?"

"It's a surprise. Close your eyes."

Dean chucked the ruined towel to the floor and leaned back against the bed. It was funny to sit here with his eyes closed, when he'd spent his life getting his kicks from having them open. Taking photos, fixing cars, getting a woman off—they were all based on him noticing things, when he'd failed to notice something essential about himself.

He'd thought he'd been keeping sex and emotions separate, but he'd been lying to himself all along. He'd been avoiding what he wanted most, thinking he was fulfilling his basic needs, but he'd had it backwards.

He was living without love. Surviving when he should've been thriving.

He should go back to school and thank his guidance counselor for making him take that art class. Shake the hand of his detention teacher. Tell them Dean Trescott finally made something of himself. But that wasn't really what he needed.

"You can open your eyes now."

She was standing by the bed, her hands empty except for her phone and a bag of Halloween candy.

"Uh, it's kinda cold out there if your plan is to have me going to this party naked."

"I thought we'd stay here instead. Just you, me and Michael."

Dean frowned. "Michael?" He knew she was kinky, but not threesome-with-one-of-his-buddies kinky.

Jamie pressed a button on her phone. Michael Jackson's "Thriller" blasted from the speaker. Dean shook his head and laughed.

"Were we ever going to a party at all?"

"Nah. It was just an excuse to make this costume for you."

Dean sat up and grabbed her, pulling her flush against him. She really was a prankster. His troublemaking fashionista jock.

"You're nuts, you know that?"

Jamie grinned. "Yeah, but that's why you like me."

"Love you," he corrected.

And there was nothing more Dean needed than that.

I hope you enjoyed *The Hierarchy of Needs*. Jamie and Dean lived right in that tension between wanting more and pretending they didn't, where good intentions and bad decisions tend to collide.

If their weekend away hooked you, frustrated you, or had you rooting for them despite themselves, I'd love to hear what you thought. Reader reviews help books like this find new readers who enjoy second chances, unresolved feelings, and chemistry that refuses to stay quiet.

If you feel like sharing, you can leave a review wherever you purchased the book, or on Goodreads. Even a few honest words make a real difference.

 *Rebecca Grace Allen*

ALSO BY REBECCA GRACE ALLEN

Legally Bound:

His Contract

Her Claim

Their Discovery

Portland Rebels:

The Duality Principle

The Theory of Deviance

Shakespeare in the City:

Taming Sugar

Hunter Pains

Decades Duet:

Find the Cost of Freedom

Smells Like Teen Spirit

EXCERPT FROM THE
THEORY OF DEVIANCE

"I say we make this interesting," Rafe said. "Usual rules, except when you bump someone's pawn back to start, you get to ask that person a question. Same if you land on a slide that's not your own color."

"What types of questions are we asking?" she asked.

"Any kind you want." The southern drawl Rafe tried so hard to hide slipped out on the letter i. He shuffled the cards. "Everybody choose your pawns."

She chose blue while Mikey picked green and Rafe decided on red. They each drew cards and made moves. Krissy was the first to bump Rafe back to home.

She did a little victory dance in her seat. "How old are you?"

He rolled his eyes. "You know the answer to that."

"Yeah, but Mikey doesn't."

Another eye roll was coupled with a shake of Rafe's head. "I'm twenty-seven." He chucked a card at Krissy. "Make your next question less boring."

They each drew cards again, and Krissy groaned when Rafe sent her pawn to the starting point.

"What was the first thing you said to me when you got back from your visit here?" he asked.

She squeezed her eyes shut. "I hate you."

"That's not what you said."

"I said I loved Maine."

"Liar, liar, pants on fire," Rafe sang.

She opened her eyes, grabbed a yellow pawn from the box, and threw it at him. He laughed and caught it. "Come on, Krissy. You can't lie during the game of Sorry."

"Otherwise known as The Game That Screws Krissy Over."

She turned to face Mikey and sighed. "I told him I thought I'd finally found someone who got me."

Mikey bumped her shoulder with his. "So did I."

A thrill went through her, bringing back the memory of his mouth on hers. On her next turn, Krissy was able to skid her pawn along a green slide. She shifted Mikey's way and leaned close enough to whisper, "Did you want to kiss me yesterday in the truck?"

"Yeah," he whispered back.

"Hey!" Rafe hollered. "No keeping secrets during Sorry."

Mikey pinched his lips together, amusement in his eyes. "Sorry, not sorry."

The two men exchanged friendly looks, seeming for the first time like they felt comfortable around each other. It made Krissy's body hum with an energy better than any drug. She reached for a card, cheering when she saw the word Sorry printed across it, and knocked one of Rafe's pawns back home.

He stared at her. "It was my turn, Krissy."

Her shoulders lifted with her giggle. "Oops."

They continued playing, chasing each other around the game board. All but one of Krissy's pawns had made it to safety when Rafe pulled a card that let him skate across a blue slide. He sat back and pursed his lips while she waited for her question.

"What's your favorite sex act?" he asked.

She narrowed her eyes at him, her cheeks going hot. "Can I veto this question?"

Rafe chuckled. "No."

She glared at him, but what the hell? This wasn't the worst thing she had to admit by far. "Being fingered. I'm boring, I guess."

Mikey cleared his throat, then shifted so his knee nudged hers. "You couldn't be boring if you tried."

The small touch made her shiver, the compliment making her face flare even hotter.

"Awww," Rafe said. "You guys are so cute."

He nudged her other knee, prodding her closer to Mikey, and the double points of contact made her skin tingle. The fantasy that had driven her over the edge last night came flooding back, and Krissy had to clench her hands into fists to stave off the torrent of images, old ones and new: Them touching her. Her touching them.

Them touching each other.

Her next move gave her a chance to ask Mikey another question, but she couldn't think clearly. "Can I pass?"

"No way," Rafe said. "We'll default to a version of the last inquiry." His grin was pure evil when he turned to Mikey. "So, Mr. Pelletier. What's your favorite sexual position?"

Shit. "You don't have to answer that," Krissy assured him.

"Yeah he does. Rules are rules."

The look Krissy threw Rafe's way clearly said shut up, but he wasn't backing down. "Come on, Mikey. Fess up. Krissy won't care if it's dirty. But remember, you've gotta tell the truth."

Mikey's voice was low when he said, "I don't have a favorite, because I haven't done it."

It wasn't often that Rafe was stunned into silence, but that did the trick.

"Oh...damn." He let out a nervous laugh. "Sorry, Mikey. Didn't mean to put you on the spot there."

Mikey didn't answer. Krissy turned the tables on her roommate.

"What about you?" she asked, arms crossed in a challenge. She knew Rafe's sensitive spots, but since actual intercourse was sexuala-non-grata, this was information that had eluded her.

"I'm not the one who lost their turn," he said. "You don't get to ask me a question."

"Don't care. Answer it anyway."

He smiled broadly, then conceded. "It depends on who I'm with. With girls I like to be on top. With guys, I prefer bottoming."

"Wait, so you're..." Mikey started, his eyes wide.

"Bi." Rafe's verification came out so matter-of-factly, typical of an actor who was confident in his sexuality and his looks. It was not typical, however, of someone who'd been through what he had. "Krissy didn't tell you?"

"No," Mikey replied stiffly, and Krissy reached for her pawns. Rafe's intentions with the game were finally clear. He was going to use it to worm out the truth and broadcast it like a billboard in Times Square.

"This is a dumb game," she said. "Let's play something else."

Rafe threw an arm out to stop her. "You're just saying that because you're losing."

He reached for a card, and his move bumped her last piece backward. He flicked the card a few times before dropping it in the pile.

"What was that fantasy you told me about? The one involving Mikey."

Even with only their knees touching, Krissy felt Mikey go rigid. She was pretty sure he could feel the same from her.

"You know the answer to that," she said, but there wasn't the same mirth in her tone as there had been when Rafe had said it.

"Mikey doesn't."

Krissy crossed her arms. Stared up at the ceiling, then at her lap. She wanted to lie, desperate to cover up the truth, but there was that burning, hungry part of her that didn't want to hide, and Rafe probably wouldn't let her anyway.

"Having a threesome," she admitted quietly. "With both of you."

Rafe sat back on the couch and slinked an arm around her.

"What do you say, Mikey? Want to help me make Krissy's fantasy a reality?"

About the Author

Rebecca lives in southern Florida with three cats who firmly believe they are the main characters. When she's not immersed in fictional love stories, she can usually be found chasing strong coffee, good workouts, and the kind of books that balance heart, heat, and humor. She writes romance for readers who like their happily ever afters earned, their characters flawed, and their love stories a little messy in the best possible way.